Snow Man

;

CAROLYN CHUTE

Snow Man

HARCOURT
BRACE &
COMPANY
NEW YORK
SAN DIEGO
LONDON

Library of Congress Cataloging-in-Publication Data
Chute, Carolyn.
Snow man/Carolyn Chute.—1st ed.
p.   cm.
ISBN 0-15-100390-4
I. Title.
PS3553.H87S56   1999
813'.54—dc21   98-35539

Designed by Linda Lockowitz
Text set in Joanna
Printed in the United States of America
First edition
E D C B A

Acknowledgments

CORK AND JANE, of course.

And thank you, Kevan Welch, whose unconditional welcome made this little book happen, and to Feeney and Mary and Susan and also to the "night screamer"; and to the late Sheriff Hayfield of Parsonsfield, Maine, whose dutiful spirit is played here by Duane.

And thank you to Peter Kellman: historian, visionary, and professional troublemaker.

And to Dr. Suzanne "D." and Dr. Mark Beever, veterinarians extraordinaires, for their kind assistance.

And to Dr. John Matthew. Thanks *again*.

And to Hy and Colleen Wald, for giving hope.

And to David Wilkinson, for the Spirit.

And to Cathy Gleason, Katherine Booker, and Roberta Record, for making *everything* possible. Helene Mekis, too. And Mark Hanley. And, of course, Everett Moulton who *is* everything possible.

And to my mother, Anne Penny, and my daughter Joannah Bowie, because we have always been able to laugh together.

And to Robyn Rosser and Steve Kelley. And Richard

Grossman. And Ward Morehouse, Carole Taylor, and Bill Corlette and Wacky Kathy and Brett. They give renewed hope. Alone there is struggle. But organized, there is resistance.

And to the MacDowell Colony. Good-bye, Bill Gnade. Good-bye, Louise Talma. Good-bye, Art. This heart misses you.

And to all of those who worked so hard to make the Wicker Beaver Festival possible.

And to my husband, Michael Chute, patient man.

And to John Sieswerda, friend and advisor.

And to my friends Jim and Vi, Joe and Mack and Sarah. Courage and kindness.

And to all of the 2nd Maine Militia and Border Mountain Militia, our militias of common sense and common decency the no-wing way.

And to my friends Ray Luc Levasseur, who is in sensory-deprivation prison in Colorado, and Tony Ford on death row in Texas, indomitable spirits no one can torture into submission although it is certainly being tried. And to all those "buried alive" in prisons by this government.

And to all revolutionaries—past, present, and future—who give everything in order that We-the-People of this tired old planet can remain free of tyranny.

It is my deepest wish that the left, right, and all in between stop pointing horizontally when they say "enemy" but to look up to that faceless elite. Unity of the People can be a formidable thing, ready to declare ourselves, ready to govern ourselves.

And to Noam Chomsky and Howard Zinn. Our teachers.

Thank you.

Author's Note

THE BOOK I've been working on since 1993 is long. A lot of characters. A lot of events. This is not that book. As you can see. It's kind of a short book.

The other book, the big one, is called *The School on Heart's Content Road*, and I don't expect it'll be smoothed out and polished and feather-dusted for a few more months as of this writing. The story has been done for a couple, three years, but polishing takes time when the book is a long one. And polishing is important. Remember what Mark Twain said: "The difference between the right word and the wrong word is like the difference between lightning and the lightning bug."

Another thing about these two books, *The School on Heart's Content Road* and *Snow Man*, is that they are related. The night after I finished one of the semipolished drafts of *Heart's Content*, I saw the scenes to *Snow Man* unfold as if the main character, Robert Drummond, had stepped right from the final scenes of that larger book. So *Snow Man* is actually a kind of DNA of the larger book. I have told many people that I was writing a book that was the "true story" of the "Militia Movement" in New England as I have experienced it. This would be the long book, *Heart's Content*. *Snow Man*, though related, is not the true story of the New England Militia Movement. It is a *possible* story, given the situation of most working Americans today, but it is not representative of the goals of the New England Militia Movement. *Snow Man* is about Robert Drummond and the family of Senator Jerry Creighton and about what happens when the "left" and the "right" come together, heart to heart.

Snow Man

Loyal to my country all the time
and to the government when it deserves it.

—Mark Twain

1

OCTOBER AFTERNOON. Barroom in Boston, Massachusetts. Bulletin comes on the TV. Senator Kip Davies is dead. He was shot execution style in the lobby of an old Boston hotel. The men responsible are an ultra-right-wing militia from Maine. Four of these men are dead, shot by Boston police. But the man who actually fired the shot into the back of the senator's head is still at large. Further details not available.

Everyone in the barroom cheers. "Get 'em all!" calls out one man. "Use a cannon!" He does not mean "get" the fleeing militiaman. He means Congress.

Another guy says, "Yuh, but execution style is kinda ..." He shivers. "Brrrr."

"Yeah. It'd be better if they just sneak up on 'em and do it humane," suggests another.

"I don't give a shit," snarls the first man, tapping his cigarette on the ashtray between himself and the guy on the next stool. "They can tar an' feather 'em. Boil 'em. Roast 'em. Don't matter. Long as they get the bastards."

"Watch out," another man cautions him. "I heard of a

guy who was arrested and put away for saying that kinda thing. An' he was just a poor old retarded guy almost eighty years old."

"This is America. I speak my mind."

In barrooms and living rooms and dooryards and workplaces all over America, people discuss the senator's demise, followed by awkward discussions of the dangers of speaking one's mind.

VENING NEWS. A face. Not a police mug shot but a somewhat fuzzy Instamatic-type home photo. This is the man authorities believe assassinated Senator Kip Davies in the lobby of the Parker House in Boston, Massachusetts, following the senator's brief address at the Fleet Center earlier that evening. The man the FBI is seeking is forty-four-year-old Robert Daniel Drummond, member of the Snow Men, an ultra-right extremist armed militia from Maine that has kept fairly quiet until now. Drummond is five feet ten inches tall, weighs about 170 pounds, dark hair, full mustache, brown eyes, wearing a camouflage uniform shirt with the patch of his militia, which figures a white Bigfoot-type beast. Screen shows this patch, probably one taken from the shirt of one of the dead members. Reportedly, Drummond is suffering a gunshot wound to the right shoulder. He is armed and considered extremely dangerous.

The home picture shows him looking uncomfortable, probably not liking a camera pointed at him, but dutifully looking into the lens with smiling eyes and a strained smile—not a big enough smile to show his teeth, just an "OK, I'm smiling" smile. There is a whiteness behind him that is either snow or a refrigerator, but you can't tell in this cropped version of the picture.

FTERNOON. Gorgeous and chill. Off Beacon Hill, Boston.

A man enters "the Stable" and begins going through drawers under a heaped workbench. He is dressed in a khaki shirt and jeans. Gray haired, fit, light on his feet. He makes a noise with his tongue and teeth. Not whistling. More like a kazoo. Something like the theme song of a movie. Something from TV.

This "Stable" used to really be a stable, for carriage horses, carriages and tack, and hay, but now it is a workshop and storage for maintenance and grounds work to the Creighton home. And it serves as a garage for two Mercedes, a Porsche, and one fire-engine-red 1966 Shelby Mustang. But it is still called "the Stable."

The stable and the home are both brick, 1700s Revolutionary era, and it being one of those perfect October days with maples yellow and the sky a roiling brew of cold lavender and gray while the sun makes sporadic orange light on everything, these brick buildings of a deep, meaty red are warm on one side, cold on the shadow side.

The maples are huge, shaggy, haughty. No oaks. Those are messy. But some fine blue spruce and one die-hard elm. Small oriental garden of herbs and dwarf fruit trees, a few shriveled vines remain of harvested veggies. Rich mosses. Wrought-iron fence. A bit of a backyard. Front yard barely. Just a quiet well-manicured strip, two spruces bunched at the right corner, and a low blue-green hedge with the tall, handsome iron fence separating it from the sidewalk. Home of Senator Jerry Creighton. Famous as "the Liberal." Though as everyone knows, the senator isn't home here these days. He's home in Washington, D.C., or off on some senatorial mission, go go go go, part of the job. Though as a successful corporate lawyer, he was never home here much then, either.

A younger man now shuffles into the Stable. White pants scuffed and splattered. Baseball shirt with rings around the shoulders in the same color as the number 44 on his back. Hair short on top, long curls in back, the fashion. Glasses of a metal frame. He stares at his shadow moving ahead there. His mind is not on the shadow, not on the raking he's been doing all day for two days, not on the beautiful day. His mind is not even in Boston. This is Mark McNaulty. The new man here.

The other man, the gray-haired one, that's Art Berry. Caretaker here for years uncountable.

"Mark! Mark!" This is coming from the open door of the storage area. It's a kind of whispered yell.

Mark looks with interest toward the open door.

"Mark! Quick!"

Mark shuffles into the storage area. No sign of Art. Just bags of Ice Melt and a new dishwasher in a crate. He steps around a high stack of screens and sees Art scooched over something, his bottom half facing the something, but he's turned at the waist, looking back at Mark, and his gray eyes are on Mark's face and the gray eyes are wild. "Ready to believe this?!"

Mark gives the nosepiece of his glasses a preparatory shove and squeezes between more stuff—big compressor, a rack of clay plant pots—and now sees there by Art's left work boot, the work boot of another man and a raised knee. A man lying on his back between stacks of green-painted wooden lawn chairs and the never-used side-bay door. Mark sees that Art's face isn't the old casual ho-hum, good-natured, an-answer-for-everything Art that he has known for nearly a year. Art looks bonkers. Flushed. Switched on. Mark steps closer to get a look at the face of the prone man, sees blood everywhere. Plopped in red-brown greasy-looking daisy shapes around on the cement, and there a zigzagging stain running along the natural grain of the plank floor, a small-scale dried-up blood Mississippi. And more brown gummyish splats coming from a stall behind him. And a fingered pool, red, gathered from under the guy's arm. Kinda sickening. The chest of the guy's camo shirt is black and brown with blood, fresh blood and yesterday's blood and blood from the day before, a jellyish mess of congealed blood, body fat, shirt fabric, and pus. The guy is breathing slow and hard. Dying. His complexion is like white soap. He's not comatose. But he's not "with it." He doesn't answer when Art goes all the way down on one knee and declares in a voice not ordinarily this squeaky and funny, "Robert! You're Robert, aren't you?! Bob! Hey, Bob!?"

Young Mark steps closer now but doesn't squat down to get that intimacy Art has with the dying man. Mark just jams both hands in his pockets and murmurs, "What the hell's he doin' here?"

Now there's the low purr of a Porsche pulling up outside, the clank of the iron gates behind it. The Porsche stops out under the trees beyond this very wall. Now there's the yap of a small dog. "Yap-yap! Yap-yap! Yap-yap! . . ." This is Duane: silver gray, streaked with peach. Black muzzle and ears, short black legs, small quick feet. Gray cheek ruffs like a midget version of Wile E. Coyote. And now a young woman's voice, soft and a little deep, a little managerial, alternating between Duane's high hard-on-the-ears yaps. This is Kristy, the senator's daughter, not a little child anymore, but a grown-up professional person who came home a few days ago to Boston to visit with her mother, who has also been here in Boston for some reason, no one knows the reason, but Kristy's real reason is to heal from something. Not a bad marriage. She has not been married. Not from a "relationship," either. It is something more lofty than just good or bad love.

Duane is outside the never-used side-bay door now, digging it to splinters, yapping, meaning to enter. Dogs love blood and pus, as we all know.

Mark speaks to the back of Art's gray head. "Uh-oh."

Now outside there Duane is suddenly quiet. And Kristy's voice is calling, "Duane! Duane! Get back here! Duane! Come, Duane!" And she whistles sharply.

Duane comes skidding around a stack of wooden screens from the front bay.

Then when Kristy Creighton comes striding long-leggedly into this storage room, she finds Mark standing there with Duane in his arms and Art standing behind him, both looking too earnestly nonchalant, and Duane twisting, grunting, trying to get free.

Kristy laughs. "Duane! Act like a gentleman."

And she reaches for the cairn terrier, who is struggling even more fiercely, and in trying to manage a grip on him, she gets a grip on Mark's oversize baseball shirt and Duane falls to the cement—"Umph!"—lands hard on his side, jerks to his feet, snakes between the men's ankles, now yapping, yapping, *Stranger! Stranger! Blood! Blood! And goo!* And then Kristy sees the dying man.

"Oh gosh!"

Even her exclamations are soft and a little hoarse, like her mother's voice, though her mother's voice is low and hoarse and loud. "What happened?"

For one moment, she puts both hands up and turns her face down and sideways as if there were a fast oncoming car, then she immediately drops down to a limber squat and lays her hand, without fear, on the middle of the man's slowly heaving stomach, the only part of his shirt not stiffened or gooey, so that now her hand rises up and down. She finds the shirt to be as hot as though freshly ironed. And she looks into the fevered man's face, his eyes glazed with the hard work of dying, the shine of his not-quite-closed eyes, his open mouth with its tongue working in and out, drawing in the cold stone-damp air of this fine historical building, of this golden October late afternoon, and of the ghastly stench of his own infection. And Duane, making about fifteen lightning-fast circles per minute around and around, also sniffs the air, yapping with a mixture of warning and wild pleasure.

Mark and Art watch Kristy hard, waiting for her to say,

"Call the police. This is the monster they are looking for."

But Kristy is not a TV watcher like Mark and Art. She's not much for the papers, either, at least lately. She does not know this face and makes no connections between "the gunshot wound to the shoulder" and the camo shirt and the murdered senator, Kip Davies. Perhaps because Kristy has so many large, noisy personal circumstances that prevent her from giving a shit about dead senators, as long as her dad is not the dead senator.

Kristy says softly, "Who is he? Why . . . ? What happened?" Then with no answers forthcoming, "I'll get an ambulance." And she stands up quickly, snatching up Duane under one arm. "Stop it, Duane!" she scolds as he thrashes against her fine suede jacket.

And Art says, "Would you do me a favor, Kristy?"

Kristy has already taken two long strides, noisy with the clomping heels of her cowboy boots—such a very long-legged and lithesome young person; she turns back, a gainly dancer's pivot.

"Don't call anyone," advises Art.

Kristy frowns, raising a dark eyebrow. "Oh?"

Art says, "This is the guy they're all after. This guy gets an ambulance straight to the electric chair or death table or whatever cute little device it is they intend to plug in. And I been thinking I can't do that to anybody. And your dad is against all that fry-'em shit and would probably agree that we need to go another route here. We need to give this another few minutes of deep thought."

Kristy's eyes are blue, interesting eyes. Beautiful and dark-lashed, yes, but also interesting. Not haughty. Not sullen. But easily affronted. Edgy. Her gaze sweeps back to the dying man and she stares.

Art asks, "You with me, Kristy?"

She sighs, "Yes."

Art rubs his face, his hair, his face again. Hard. He says, "Jesus Christ."

Mark wonders, "So whatta we gonna do?"

Kristy bows her head, her face in Duane's fur, her eyes squinched as if trying to stop a dream she doesn't like.

Mark pesters, "So, shit, whatta we gonna do?"

Art throws up a hand, traffic-cop style. "Wait! Everyone calm down!" And yet he himself seems the most distressed.

Kristy says tightly, "He looks awful. There's nothing we can do."

Art throws up his hand again. "Everyone calm down!"

Mark asks, "We gonna hide him?"

Art paces once, one hand on his head. "Well, I know one thing. He's gotta come up off that floor. We gotta find somebody . . . some doctor."

Kristy opens her mouth to speak. Looks like a protest.

"But what we need right now is to stay calm!" Art commands. "And give this some deep thought. This . . . is . . . somethin' we gotta think about. Right?"

Kristy's face looks pretty stony, pretty hard, pretty unaccommodating. But she speaks softly, "He looks so sick."

Art proposes, "How 'bout we find someone somewhere . . . to fix him and give us more time to figure out what in hell we're going to do?" He paces around once again, now facing Mark.

Mark says quickly, "I know a vet."

Art looks at Mark's mouth speaking this interesting concept. "Vet?"

"Yep. He's a good shit."

"He could lose his license," Kristy warns.

"We could all lose our licenses," Art says with a little ugly chuckle.

Kristy strokes Duane, who has stopped struggling. Deep in her neck, a little squeak, like a misdirected swallow or cry. She murmurs, "This is frightening."

Mark persists, "I bet Woody would fix him up and not tell. He's ... hot shit. I've known him for ages. He's ... calm as a cookie. Nothing fazes him. I've known him for eons."

Kristy stares at the dying man. Duane, beginning to struggle again, stares at the dying man. Art and Mark stare at the dying man.

Kristy now steps over the dried river of blood and does something with her feet with those pointy-toed, glossy cowboy boots. Looks like she's about to kick the guy, but she's just almost lost her balance, Duane's weight making her top-heavy. She stares unblinkingly down at the man's face, the dark mustache, the straight nose. A striking man. Even while dying. Like a movie star dying on the screen. Only movie stars never really master that terrible glazed look of death or near-death. The foolish lack of dignity, the way the tongue takes such energy just before lolling loosely like a strip of pale raw fish. And movie stars never smell green and ghastly. She says, "Yes, there's serious consequences for those who aid and abet ... or harbor ... or whatever that is ... especially ... with ... with this guy." She touches the man's thigh with her boot toe.

Mark looks ready. He nods rapidly. "I'll go get Woody."

Kristy is doing an odd thing. She keeps pushing the

man's thigh with her boot toe. This is not the guy's leg that is raised with the knee against the bay door, but the other leg, and as she keeps at it, the toe of his work boot rocking sensuously from side to side, Robert Drummond shows no sign of this bothering him. Then Kristy says in her low, soft, hoarse voice, "Take him in through the pantry," and Mark and Art waste no time, squatting down to deal with the dead weight of their patient, trying to find the right grip.

The sick man's right hand opens and closes, his eyes open, he speaks harshly, "Don't!" and grimaces, and he gets really stiff in the back and legs, maybe trying somewhere in the fog of his dim consciousness to stand, and then through the pantry he speaks again, "Awrrrrr! Stop that!!!" And then there is the gee-hawing struggle up the two flights of stairs to the third floor. As they lay him on the lemon-yellow spread of the twin bed by one of the dormers filled with books and glass pretties and pumpkin-colored October light, there in the large third-floor "study room," he speaks again, "Get away," and grimaces and raises the knee of his right leg again, which makes him look casual and contented.

Art says to Mark, "Go get Woody." And Mark heads down the two flights of stairs, bursting through the rooms and hallways and the pantry large as anyone else's living room, and to his truck, revs the engine, gets it in gear, slams the door, and backs all the way out through the slowly opening gates to the bright street.

THE VETERINARIAN is young, tall, thin, with a lot of Adam's apple. Blond. Sweet girlish flush and hands as steady as iron. He has carried in two book satchels. A green one. And a black one. The kind bookstores give out for advertisement. In the room just below, Duane yaps, and probably the vet notices this and wonders at how life takes odd twists sometimes.

The vet is tugging on a pair of surgical gloves before he gets within two feet of his patient. His name is Dr. Kenneth Wood. He is kindly. And he is, yes, calm as a cookie. And he is honest. "I'd say Robert is very sick. This is a serious infection. His fever...it could already have caused permanent...problems for Robert. This is a high fever. And he has lost a lot of blood. I have no way of getting him the blood he needs...human blood. I'm really sorry." He speaks this as he almost lovingly probes the shoulder and ribs through the gummy, crusty fabric of the camo shirt.... This probing, which sets the patient off—a long groan, nearly a sob, then a warning, "Get the fuck away"; he then starts to get up, eyes open, then covers his eyes with the forearm of his uninjured arm and goes back down again, both legs bent at the knee now. His eyes are closed. But he's not relaxed. He's braced. The vet waits patiently, showing no irritation or surprise at this.

Now the vet casually unbuttons the camo shirt with its patch of an abominable hairy white beast on the sleeve. The patient seems OK about this. Underneath this shirt is a black T-shirt with a leather shoulder holster and a .357 Magnum revolver with dark handgrips, this against the ribs on the right side. The vet reaches for scissors, and Kristy and Art and Mark watch him cut away strips of the bloodied camo fabric. And then he removes the holster and heavy firearm tenderly, hangs gun and holster over the bedpost, all the while softly explaining that there can be bone shards, nerve damage to the arm ... a lot of X rays needed, a surgeon and operating room equipment and an anesthesiologist and staff ... and blood. But he says he can clean the wound, stitch it up, stop the bleeding, get antibiotic into him, and try to get his temperature down. He asks Kristy how much ice might be available. Any ice packs ... find them fast. And try to get this room temp down a little. He promises that when he leaves here he'll try to locate some IV fluids and something that will build the man's blood. But he repeats, "Robert is very sick."

And as he speaks, Robert's tongue and jaws work, drawing the air that smells of nice rugs and good books and wicker and leather and cold, unused scented candles, and other sweet and delicate things that belong to Kristy here in her attic apartment, the set of rooms she spent her teenage years in, studied in, dreamed in. Dark-haired, lanky Kristy Creighton, growing, achieving, becoming.

The doctor cuts away the black T-shirt, all the while speaking softly to those in the room as he would to the distressed owners of a dying dog, and sometimes he speaks to Robert, who is much looser now, one bent leg flopped over now, and the doctor says, "OK, Robert, here goes," speaking to his patient in the way he always must, the words the patient never understands, but the voice the patient always trusts.

A stethoscope swings from the doctor's gloved fingers and is now pressed to the we'whomp we'whomp we'whomp, which no one but him hears. He has no comment on the heart but glances over at his friend Mark and says, "His fever is very high: Very high. Prolonged high fever . . . it's bad. We need to talk about the possibility of seizures. I'm thinking maybe we could put him on the floor on the mattress . . . in case. And we do need to get the ice cubes . . . They can be placed in plastic bread bags or freezer bags. And towels . . . we'll need a dozen towels." And he asks for three straight-back chairs, and there's the scurrying of people fulfilling all these needs. Now upon two of the newly arrived chairs he sets up his instruments and containers of gauzes and antiseptics. The third chair he straddles while peeling off the messy latex gloves, dropping them into a bag, and smooths on another pair. He explains that Robert will probably resist when he cleans the wound, so would Mark or Art get a grip on the patient's left arm and hand? He offers a pair of surgical gloves. Art steps up to the bed. The light of the dormer window is both bright enough for surgery and beautiful. Light of the spirit.

Nobody speaks, but everyone's eyes are fixed on the tattoos tumbling up and down both of Robert

Drummond's darkly but softly haired arms lying across several towel-covered pillows of ice. There on the left forearm, a tattoo of a sun with an old calendar-style face and an aureole of stiff, twisted corkscrew flames. Bright preschool yellow inside lines of uncompromising black. A fine and eloquent masterpiece. The way some of your to-day's tattoo artists take themselves seriously. Artistes!

And above the sun tattoo, probably an older one . . . a simple Christmas tree, the balsam, as it might look on a road sign or forest products packaging. A kind of friendly green.

While above the tree on the bicep and nearly to the shoulder, a gray-blue wrinkly-kneed elephant toting an American flag in its upraised trunk. The tiny flag is splotchy with color—errors—the red-and-aqua-blue stripes a little botched. Errors not so easy to repair. And across the elephant's body, the letters GOP.

Meanwhile, almost all of Robert's right arm is a show-case of color. A long-torsoed, very red devil. The tattoo artist responsible for this one was also very gifted. Has mastered the look of cold, unfeeling evil on the devil's bearded face. Pitchfork in one hand. While grasped in the other is what looks like a new baby at first, held by the feet, screaming. But it's really a small naked man. The devil is thoroughly and happily embroiled in flames that frisk and billow around him and then up over him into the heavens, which are actually Robert's shoulder and col-larbone and throat, great seething ribbons and tongues of purple, scarlet, and yellow orange. But the garbagey mess of the infected exit wound and its purpled fingers and clouds of bruise have erased much of this beatific inferno forever.

Meanwhile the devil himself is unscathed. See there! His yellow eyes are keen!

And there down on the top of the wrist, last but not least, a small blue swastika.

All this storm of color against skin that looks as bloodless as paraffin.

Duane is quiet now, locked up in that room below. Listening hard. Duane is the kind of individual who never rests. He knows certain laws exist, certain principles, which he was put on earth not to make, but to enforce. Presently his head is cocked, his eyes bright with duty.

Nearly an hour passes with the clinks of instruments, the quiet work of cleaning and stitching, and the vet's soft, honest voice and now and then a troubled moan from Robert Drummond or a bit of thrashing and garbled curses at Art, who has a serious grip on his arm, curses that eventually subside. Robert Drummond who is unanesthetized but "very sick." As gauze is finally laid over stitches and pink jellyesque areas of open fat and muscle, the vet points out the bloody jeans and bloody work boots that Robert still wears and tells the group, "I'll leave you a box of these gloves. Don't touch any of this blood. Get rid of these clothes. Get rid of this bedding." He nods to the yellow bedspread, which is spotted bright and brownish with blood and other yellows, those of infection, and the brown of iodine.

Mark says, "Damn! I got some on me when we lugged him in!"

The vet says, "Yes, And I noticed a spot of it on the pantry-way floor coming in." He hands Mark a sterile wipette. "Here. Do your hands with these." Hands him another. "Use bleach on the floors where you find spots.

Bleach your clothes when you get home, Mark. Everything will be fine." He then winks at Art. "There are some things I learned today. And that is not to get excited and go off and leave things. After all, who knows? I might need to do this again. Maybe I can start a new career. Doctor of Fugitive Medicine." He winks again, this time at Kristy, who misses it because she is staring at Robert. Her face is tight.

Mark is squinting at his friend Woody. What, Woody excited? Went off and forgot things? Not possible.

Placing his surgical gloves in a plastic bag with the rest of the mess of the procedure, the vet speaks into Mark's eyes, "When he dies and you call the law to come get his body, just tell him you found him the way he is. They won't believe you." He looks now at Kristy. "They'll know things don't add up. But maybe...they like your father or something."

Kristy looks at him. She says coldly, "Don't worry. Your name won't come up. They can pull my tongue out. OK?"

The doctor almost flushes.

Then Kristy almost flushes. "I'm sorry, Doctor. I thank you for taking this risk. We've all been unwise. I never thought I'd be faced with ..."

Art interrupts, "If it was just jail ... but they go so friggin' far, the goddamn sonsa bitches." Art looks quickly at Kristy. "Excuse me."

She looks mightily irritated by this apology that singles her out.

While everyone talks urgently and softly, the vet slips on another pair of gloves and finds Robert's wallet, flipping through it, stares a moment at something, then leaves the wallet on the window seat. He stares a long moment at the wallet lying there, the fingertips of his gloved left hand touching those of his right.

The others whisper, whisper, whisper, some gentle argument going on.

Now slowly the vet tugs away his gloves, finger by finger. Clears his throat. And that's when they all look at him and he speaks almost sheepishly, "I'll come by tonight. It'll take a few hours to track down what I need to get for Robert. I can't get human blood. I'm sorry. And I can't operate on his shoulder." He smiles wanly. "And I'm ashamed to say that in the rush, I didn't pack a thermometer so I can't say exactly what Robert's temperature is . . . but when someone's too hot to touch, we say for sure he's in trouble." Now his voice changes, less rote and professional, less apologetic, less easygoing. "A bit of advice. Hide the gun. He might use it on you. He's helpless now . . . but . . . if he lives . . . he's going to pick up where he left off."

All of Robert's saviors look at him sharply.

There's a thump and a very mean tearing sound . . . khhhhhhhhhh! khhhhhhhhhh! khhhhhhhhhhhh! Krrrrrichhhhhhhhh! in another part of the house. Color drains from everyone's faces.

Kristy murmurs, looking into each face, "I know it's probably Priss." She looks at the vet. "She's our housekeeper. She was coming back for a few minutes, something Mom wanted her to get . . . but . . ." Kristy steps up to one of the small many-paned gable windows, looks out. "I don't see her car, but she might be parked around back." She steps over to one of the back dormers, peers down.

But it's only Duane. He has nudged all the shoes and sneakers out of the senator's wife's dressing-room shelves, torn the drapes completely out of one window, pissed on the door, and there's a lamp knocked off from a little night table. His head is cocked, ears opened wide as radar dishes, listening for someone to come running to scold him. But nothing. Just those shuffling overhead feet, all absorbed in something unusual, therefore a broken law. Duane hops on the big bed now, his mind working lightning fast.

Everyone up on the third floor is nervous as hell now. Kristy assures everyone her mother won't be back till late and her father isn't expected around here for at least another week.

Now there's a really big bang! Kristy hurries downstairs to check the kitchen, pantry, hallways, dining room. She runs along opening each and every door. "Hello?" "Hello? Who's there?" At last she opens the door to the master bedroom, which is more than half of the second floor of the main part of the house, with its two bathrooms, two small dressing rooms, and a solarium over the two-story ell. And Duane, who runs at her, flings himself against her hip with a desperate grunt, and there she sees the cheerily naked window, torn drapes in a cream-colored hump on the floor. And piss on the door. And what's that? Antique 1770s brass pendulum clock now on the floor on its face ... not on top of the cabinet ... not ticking. And there, too, on the floor, facedown, her parents' wedding picture ... glass shattered. Duane throws himself at the closed door. "Forget it, Duane. Not now." She squats down a moment, let's him kiss one of her ears. Stands back up, gazing around the room, sighs.

Out on the stairway, she meets the vet. He nods. Hurries on down.

And now Mark leaving, to go home and bleach the daylights out of himself.

Back upstairs, Art tells her he will take care of undressing Robert Drummond. He glances at the guy spread-eagled on the bed; bloody jeans, bloody boots, some towel-wrapped ice-filled bread bags in place around his torso, neck, and head, making a cold nest. And on a chair, a box of surgical gloves.

Kristy stands with her hands in the pockets of her dark suede jacket, which she's still wearing though the room is stifling hot, this attic always hotter than anywhere. She loves heat. Her vacations are always to fabulous aqua blue–green water, white-beach pink-seashell islands and capes, sometimes the hot, breathless Middle East. Now her adrenaline is subsiding a bit. Reality rustles. Prickles the skin. "Well, I can certainly do this with you." She looks at Art, his thornlike short gray hair, the gathers around his mouth and Nixonlike nose. His all-is-well expression. Gray eyes that seem to age so much every time she is away. She smiles. "You know where the trash bags are." She doesn't ask this. She states it. Art has worked here, lived here at times, longer than she has. He knows where everything is and how it came to be there.

Now she hears his boots going lightly along the little landing hall, his walk always a kind of sneaky hunter's advance, bent at the knees. Never a scuff. Then the door to the stairs gives off its well-oiled whisper. Then his footsteps descending.

She turns to the bed, her pale eyes unblinking. Robert

Drummond, colorific. Tattoos in all possible hues of anguish. And the gold seepage of iodine through the gauzed-over shoulder and bicep. And the deep plum map of bruise around the gauze, blurring and mixing with the devil's bright firmament. And the towels of his ice pillows, red, ruby, forest green, and mauve. And one with yellow-and-blue sea horses. One a purple plaid. The turning of the dying afternoon sun places a contemptuous faded gold along the ribs, heaving chest, throat, and arms. She steps closer. Nothing changes. Still he pants. Slowly. What are those long spaces between? Does his fist-sized heart actually pause? And is he really gasping for air? Sounds almost more like grunts of complaint.

His tongue is thick. Tongue coated. She looks into his face, the broad, high cheeks, the half-open almond eyes and frowning dark brows ... frowning, yes. She keeps forgetting he is not unconscious, just dazed. At moments his drowsy eyes actually slide to the left or right, hovering longest on the glowing window. She surmises he is part Indian ... some Maine tribe—Penobscot, Passamaquoddy, Micmac—they have them there. Or is he Black Irish? Or both? How the human rivers make their junctions, mixing uneasily, but never receding! She sighs. He is beautiful. Those perfectly placed eyebrows, but frown lines between them, and the puckering and softening of skin under the eyes and lines beginning across his forehead, which mean he's well into his forties. Lustrous dark untrimmed mustache. A few days of beard filling in. She considers the few dozen white hairs on the chin, the rest black and red brown and glossy. "Don't die," she whispers.

She drives her knee into the side of the bed. Bed

shivers. Nothing else changes. The man still gasps, chest still rises and falls in its struggle to take in the air of this hour. Will this be his last hour?

Her mother will be home tonight, just one of her quick stops in D.C. . . . . Each visit there is quicker, less said. Her mother will not like this. Why would she? It's crazy. Kristy knows that if this happened a year ago, before the sheer speed of her complex life broke the spirited camel's back, she would have . . . yes . . . called the police.

She hears Art on the stairs returning. He swaggers into the room, a walk from the knees, hands a little fisted, a man who is sixty and still strong, still proud, so fucking working class, and she turns to him and she has tears in her eyes. And he sees this and he says, "I can put a sleeping bag down over there and spend the night. I just need to think up a good story to tell Mary." He studies Robert a long moment. "I don't want you stuck with the whole project, Kristy."

She bristles. "I can handle it."

He looks at her hard. "This could get nasty. A lotta ways it could get nasty."

She raises her chin.

"I'll show you how to use that gun," he offers quickly, walking toward where it hangs on the post.

"No!" she snaps. "I don't want that gun. Get it out of here. Take it someplace."

Art scratches the back of his neck, head cocked sideways. "I dare not drive across town with Evidence, Exhibit A. My plate light's out. No sense adding more opportunities for disaster to this ol' *Titanic* we're riding on."

"Well, will you check it? See if it's loaded or whatever and put it in my room, under the mattress?"

With relief, Art says, "Sure." He pats her shoulder. "I'm sorry." He looks back at Robert, then to her, "I got you into this."

She says, "No problem. I have only about fourteen phones in this house." She glances toward the phone-fax setup blinking with recent messages next to her computer under the slanted ceiling between the two farthest dormers. "If he tries to kill me, I'll call 911, goddamn him."

Though he doesn't seem much comforted by this 911 idea, Art says, "Okeydoke." He shakes open a black garbage bag. Ties small rabbit ears on one side so that it can hang off the back of one chair. "You ready for this, ma'dear?"

She wishes Art weren't here. It is embarrassing only because he is here. It's not like Kristy is Miss Prim. She's had three live-in lovers and, for god sakes, she's had drawing classes! But Art Berry has always been a father figure, you know, on that other plane of life. But if she asks him to leave and then in another three beats, calls him back . . . shit.

So she and Art both put on gloves. Each starting with the left hand. Then the right. Like a nice waltz. One-two. One-two.

She steps up to the bed. She unties one of Robert's blood-blackened work boots. Art, the other. They plop the boots into the bag. The socks, blue with bloodied cuffs. The feet free of blood. White and bony, nails trimmed and clean. Unruffled 1990s Kristy Creighton reaches for the belt. She jerks it from the loops, rolls it up, and places it on the wide window-seat sill. Now a jackknife. She places it with the belt. And now tinkling together deep in the other pocket, down against his hip, she finds more than a dozen gun cartridges, brass with the copper jacket, then the tip of lead and two empty shells. She arranges these on the window seat. The sun is gone now. Just the shadowy blue spruces that fill this dormer window and the restive lion color of the sunset between each limb and needle, and the black-blue silhouette of one of the across-the-street neighbors' many chimneys as seen through a gap in the spruce limbs.

She turns back to the bed and without hesitation, unsnaps the jeans, unzips them. Art grins at her as it's plain to see that Robert Drummond does not wear underwear.

And now Robert Drummond's eyes are wide open and he is looking right at Kristy, still breathing slow and hard, openmouthed, a stare, like that of a panting dog's in summer. Now his eyes turn toward the window. Now the lids droop.

Kristy lets her gloved hands slap to her sides, yes, touching her sides. She turns away.

Art says, "It's OK, Kristy—"

"I'm going to get him a shirt," she says, stupidly.

Art watches her standing there, his own gloved hands almost touching his sides.

She says, "I'm sorry. I'm not myself. This was a really bad time . . . before this. This . . . is a little much."

Art points to himself, a gesture unseen by anyone. "I am sorry. I am the one that needs to be sorry. Goddamnit. This is bad. Jesus. I'm taking all the blame, OK. And I'm going to sack out here till he's outa here."

She says nothing, just peels off her gloves, throws them into the bag, turns sharply, and strides hurriedly through the open French doors to the small parlor with it's two dormers—one west, one east—then through the kitchenette and into her bedroom. One small capable act. To find something for Robert to wear when he "wakes up." Something to warm him when he is no longer fire.

She rustles through two of her closets, a few drawers . . . everything so girlish—or, rather, womanly. Here, a shirt with buttons on the man's side, gray, black, and pink plaid. She can tell it will fit him. She has memorized Robert Drummond's person, like you memorize the door you need to get back out of to escape a dark, cackling, horns-blowing haunted house.

When she returns with the shirt, Art has done the job. Even the bedspread and blanket and top sheet are gone, and the smaller bag of waste the vet left, now all stuffed into two big trash bags, knotted up and ready by the door to the stairs. And all the towel-covered bags of ice are back in place. Kristy says nothing. No thanks. And she does not glance at Robert, still spread-eagled on the bed, a pale X in the corner of her eye.

Art looks at the plaid shirt.

She makes a little pained sound and drops the shirt over one bedpost.

"Go home," she tells Art, her voice almost spookily, suddenly managerial and focused. "If you have to tell Mary about this, that's one more person who will know . . . and you shouldn't have to lie to her. Just go home. This is actually quite good for me, Art. Especially now. This is like . . . like . . . you know those programs where they leave young kids on islands or in the wilderness to live on mushrooms and it transforms them . . . out there with all those bears and sounds and no crutches. I need this!" She smiles.

He swings his shoulders and arms a little, running this wild concept through his head.

"The gun," she reminds him.

Obediently, he lifts the thing by its leather strap, pulls the gun out, and peers into the space behind the cylinder where the rims of the cartridges show. He raises the hammer carefully with his thumb, two clicks, and flips open the gate. Then pointing the barrel up, one cartridge slips from the gate into his hand. Four more cartridges drop one at a time into his cupped right hand as he rotates the cylinder. He adds them to the rest on the window seat. He sniffs the chambers. "They say he shot the senator twice. Execution style. I would've thought once was enough."

Kristy squeezes her eyes shut.

As Art returns from her bedroom, gunless, he promises to come back in the morning early. He reminds her that Woody is coming back tonight. "Best you tell Connie and get it over with."

Kristy swallows.

He shoulders both garbage bags, says, "I'll take these down to the shop and put them in the woodstove. So if you smell funny smoke, don't wonder a thing." He stares out one gable window a moment, down the short street. "Don't forget to remind Connie that if she calls the cops, we'll all be arrested." He snorts softly. "I'm looking forward actually to your mom's take on this...her exact words." Now he turns and looks at the form on the bed, which Kristy is deliberately keeping her eyes away from. He chuckles. "Gawd, maybe she'll love 'im." He winks at Kristy and heads out toward the little hall. From the doorway he points to the dormer near Robert's bed. "Woody put his wallet over there."

In the master bedroom below, Duane listens to Art's footsteps lightly descending the various stories of the house, Art's smooth car engine heading out through the electronic gates. Gates clanging shut. Duane considers the very wrongness of all this, the way humans err . . . to err is human. Himself, he knows only right.

THE EVENING NEWS reports that security for members of Congress as well as the president and vice president and staff has been maximized, as authorities have as yet been unable to take Robert Drummond into custody.

Barrooms and workplaces and kitchens all over America are emitting little cheers of "Alll right!!"

Unmentioned on the report is the fact that Senator Kip Davies was one of those guys that even the other senators and reps didn't really like. And liking each other is what Congress is all about, sort of. Like a maggot in a brimming garbage can has to really like the other maggots. But Senator Kip Davies had a way of making Congress look bad . . . made it look to the public like it was a garbage can . . . which it is, as we said before. But, gee.

Senator Davies's fibs weren't sleek doublespeak doublethink Orwellian mind-control fibs like the ones the rest of Congress and various administrators wield with such splendor. Senator Davies's fibs were just bald-faced LIES. The kind even the average American can see through. And such a big-mouth asshole. That's the worst part. His arrogance was right up front. On his face. Big sneery, smarmy, bug-eyed, happy ol' we're-puttin'-it-to-all-you face. So at his funeral, everyone will bow their heads, and condolences to the widow will have a clearly false edge.

But the wrath toward Robert Drummond and those corpses that remain of his militia is real. Like if we let this kinda thing go on, who's next?

Then there's the practical side, the bright side. This helps pass lots more "antiterrorism" stuff like fewer court appeals for the poor, and lots and lots of antigun legislation like you can buy a Russian SKS with a bayonet, but not a Chinese SKS with a bayonet, and then you can ban certain guns and certain ammunition, which makes gun lovers buy more guns and ammo just before the bill's passage at higher prices and then underground afterward at really high prices, which makes bad people out of all the people who own these things, people who can't even conceive of a bank robbery or drive-by shooting, while the "liberal" part of the population feels safe and relieved once you tell them in a tough voice that guns will soon be out of the hands of citizens, out of all those irresponsible, violent hands!

SHE IS NOT AFRAID. He has groaned, a rather lusty groan, almost a howl, and again tried to get up off the bed, then eased back and thrashed a bit, the peach-colored sheet she had placed over him trickles over the edge of the mattress, flops to the floor. She stands up from where she has been nestled in a chair in her little living room and is trying to pay attention to a TV video with the volume low, a tape one of her students loaned her before Kristy left school abruptly, a tape called *Women Warriors*—mythical and historical, their artifacts, legends, and literature. Now she comes to stand here in the large study room with its books and computer and antique rolltop desk, a half-dozen sleepy ceramic and hardwood Buddhas, one bronze —that one on the floor against the gable wall being the size of a preteen child—and the dormers with only queer pink security lights beyond, no curtains; you'd have to be in a helicopter to see much on this third floor . . . and there, one dim amber-and-green leaded glass lamp on a low table and the guest bed with, yes, a guest in it. And the room is hot as hell and he has turned his head to one side and she sees that the damp dark hair on the back of his neck, behind the ear, is a little curly, not knucklelike curls, not ringlets. Robert's curls are just thoughtless half-hearted twists...and there she sees his aging neck, a couple of weathered-looking crisscrossing lines. As her eyes slide down his body, she feels someone watching her through every blank dim window. Not the neighbors on their roofs. Not the FBI in helicopters or trees or ladders. Not even God, whom she doesn't believe in really. But the fierce eye of Robert's guardian angel and an angelic cry of "Wrong! Wrong!"

Is this a kind of rape, to stare at the defenseless? Maybe. Would she object if it were herself sprawled out there, some guy standing over her, staring? Yessss. But there it is, the long uncircumcised penis against his leg. She hugs herself. She is holding her breath.

She hurriedly grasps the sheet from the floor and flops it over him. Some of his bags of ice are on the floor. Some still on the bed. Not many are actually still touching him. All are mostly melted and leaking. She plunges down the stairs and through the cooler rooms of the first floor for fresh ice. She holds one cube of ice to her forehead, then over her cheeks and chin. Then back upstairs she gets an armload of bedding from one of her closets. She lugs them to the dimly lit study room and heaves them onto the floor by the bed. What if he has seizures? There had been mention of putting him and the mattress on the floor. Somehow overlooked. She has heard of the real vio-lence of seizures. Jesus. Jesus. She watches his chest and stomach work through each slow, hard gasp. The tongue. The jaws. No change. No miracles of veterinary medicine here. And the gauze taped to his shoulder, the reek of its gold-brown iodine, this rises up hotly to her face. And the smell of his mouth and tongue, a kind of chemical smell, bitter and ugly. And from his hair and hands, the distinct naughty smell of cigarettes. She turns and looks at the belt and knife and the cartridges and the wallet on the window seat. She picks up the wallet and settles on one of the straight-back wooden chairs next to the bed, her knee touching the bed. She holds the wallet, worn, thick, soft. She looks back to the bed, over the long stretch of tattoos to his right hand, nothing like her ex-boyfriend Jared's hand. Nothing like Barry's hand, her boyfriend before Jared. One a chemist, one a freshman House Rep from Wyoming.

This hand of Robert's looks more like Art's. Art. Art, who in some ways has been her true father. School, ballet, modern dance, piano and flute and voice, swimming, skiing, horseback riding, museums, trips were all out there. But home was Art. And once Mary, his wife, when she was housekeeper . . . before she got her social work training and halfway-house jobs. But there was always Art. Consistent as a stone. Kristy had always stuck to him like glue. "Helping" him, getting her hands dirty, learning how to wire a lamp, making "people" out of wire with plugs for hands and feet, a lightbulb in a socket for a head . . . smiley face drawn on the lightbulb. How to kill crabgrass. How to change a furnace filter. And asking him all the big and little questions he answered so well, the little questions that seemed big and the big questions that seemed little. She sees that on Robert's left hand, he wears no wedding ring. Neither does Art. Though Art loves Mary, Art says rings are dangerous. You could lose a finger. Kristy has never heard anyone but Art say this. She flips open the wallet.

Robert does something with his mouth. Sounds like sucking. But then goes back to the same old thing, the slow draw of breath, like complaints.

Cash in the wallet. She counts out sixty-two dollars in small bills. No credit cards. Not one. But a blood donor card and a lot of business cards. Different people. Different builders. Plumbers. Electricians. Foundation outfits. Paving and seal coating. Gun shops. Trading posts. Car auction. Some cards have names, dates, or numbers scribbled on the back. One says *get back*. Another says *three lefts after pond*. And there's a folded-up invoice from a lumberyard.

A photo driver's license. Robert's face. Smiling. A big, happy, silly, boyish wise-guy grin. Same dark mustache, all the way down to the jaws, but no week's worth of beard. Collar and shoulders of a dark work shirt shows. And the white V of a T-shirt. ROBERT DANIEL DRUMMOND. BIRTHDATE: 4-24-54. HEIGHT: 5'10", WEIGHT: 170 POUNDS. Yes, so there's no mistake. It's him. Would have been nice if there'd been a mistake, a wild coincidence. She closes her eyes. She, yes, really all along had hoped for that, hadn't she? That he was not really Robert Drummond. She sighs.

Now she finds his social security card, yellowed and torn and taped. Five blue torn-in-half ticket stubs to last year's Fryeberg Fair. A dried four-leaf clover. How sweet! How ordinary. She carried one herself for years.

She wouldn't have expected pictures. But here they are. A guy on a Harley. Dark rough-looking character. A bit fat. Not Robert. School photos. Some younger, then older, of the same two kids, now teens. A boy and a girl.

They look like Robert, too much like him to be just nieces and nephews. And another cheapie-type studio shot of a little serious-looking girl. Looks like Robert. Kristy picks this one from the plastic. *Ariel, age 4.* And, yes, here's one of the wife. She looks like she could be Robert's sister. Same dark looks. Same eyes. But no. Not a sister. This is spelled out in some way on Kristy's fingertips. And here's another one, the same woman on a greenish sofa, nursing a tiny baby. Back of this picture says *Cindy and Ariel (4 days old).*

Now a piece of a larger snapshot cut to wallet size with scissors. It's of a big yellow thing. Not a tractor exactly. Has tires tall as a man. Tires meant to grip. Chains over the tires. There's a blade at one end. At the other end, cables for winching. She can't make out the driver. He's just a darkened form inside a caged-up cab. The leafless trees make bold black zebralike shadows.

The rest of the pictures are houses. All unpainted and brand-new with sandy backfill, no grass yet. Most of them are Capes. With ells. Mud rooms. Garages. A lot of windows. *Big* houses. Trophy houses. The kind that merit a picture in the wallet. Some have pioneer porches. All have impressive chimneys. Sawhorses and dismantled staging around. One shows a new but dusty truck parked close to the door of the ell. Ladders on this truck. The windows of the house are smoodged with putty, spotted with pink manufacturer's stickers.

WHEN KRISTY HEARS her mother's car pausing at the gates to wait for the electronic opener, she hurries downstairs to meet her.

Duane is yapping and racing around. A little bit of

foam rubber in the hall. Another decimated pillow. He's not himself. He, who usually gets to be with Kristy upstairs when the rest of the great house is empty. He, who, for reasons he knows but can't speak, has been kept downstairs. He races to meet Connie, head woman of the house, yapping, looking back over his shoulder toward the door to the stairs, stairs that go up, yapping, moving like lightning around Kristy, making a circle around her like the red marks around errors Connie used to make on students' papers years ago when she taught school in France for a time.

Connie Creighton is laughing. "Duane! Calm down! Get your wits about you! It's just me!" Her laugh is deep and a little burlesque.

And then Kristy murmurs, "Mom?" And she falls against her mother, crying.

"What, sweetie? What?"

"I don't know!" Kristy wails. "I think I'm going crazy!"

"Well, it's OK. Let's get settled in here a minute and talk." Connie takes off her light jacket, flomps her high-society big-brimmed hat on the entryway's antique 1770s high-backed bench.

"Mom . . . it's big. It's a big, big problem. And . . . it . . . it's upstairs."

Duane looks toward the stairs, a word he knows well, but laden with extraspecial meaning now. He scuttles over to the door to the stairs, yapping, his tail spinning, hurries back. Yes! Yes! Upstairs! Hurry! In his head, sirens, alarms, flashing lights. In his eyes twinkles of purpose and duty about to be fulfilled.

THE SENATOR'S WIFE, Constance Creighton, begins to yell in a fashion unbecoming to the neighborhood in which they live, and yet not out of character for Constance herself, for she is not a soft-spoken edgy person like her daughter, nor smooth and restrained like her husband. So she yells, "What were you thinking!!!!!!" and Duane yaps and races around, eyes twinkling, happy to have the rest of the Force here at home at last. As Connie yells, here upstairs in Kristy's apartment—two rooms away from "the problem"—"the problem" groans and draws up his right leg, and the sheet slides off that thigh and off his hip and the fabric pools in a more dense peach-colored pile over his genitals.

"Your father's political career could be smashed! His opponents would only need to hint that perhaps that man in the other room was hired by your dad . . . and the public would believe it! Even if the FBI knew it was ridiculous, the public does not know what is ridiculous!"

Kristy weeps, hunkered on the edge of the pretty little oak chair in her very modern not-at-all 1770s kitchenette, her forehead against the knuckles of her slim right hand.

Now Connie gets very quiet. Deathly quiet. Duane has stopped yapping but sniffs excitedly at the closed study-room doors. A car slows outside, stopping at a neighbor's gate. A jet thunders overhead, dragging itself westward. The rest of the world, oblivious to the ridiculous, the rest of the world creaking along in its happy humdrum, in its proud innocence.

And now, yes, real silence. Horrid silence.

Kristy hears chuckling. Evilish chuckling. She raises her head, sees that, yes, her mother is really chuckling. And now this mother beams. "And my god...my god in the heavens! Your father is a Democrat!" She shakes her head violently, shakes her cheeks, eyes squinched shut. Then, "That is, weeeee are Democrats, Kristina. We are good Democrats...flawless...impeccable Party persons...loyal to the marrow!" She throws out an arm. Stares with great feeling at a spot high on the wall.

Kristy sniffs back tears, pushes her nose childlike against the top of her classy blue shirtsleeve. "I know it," she murmurs cautiously.

Connie slaps both of her thighs, then reaches across and pokes one of Kristy's knees. And now this mother begins to really hoot in earnest. Gagging laughter. This is not out of character for her. Those in the know know that Senator Jerry Creighton's wife, Constance, is nothing like the practiced plastic professional Hillary Clinton type nor the garden-club Barbara Bush type, nor the regal Nancy Reagan type. Could there be a slot in political circles for a Broadway type?

Now Connie and Kristy are laughing madly together, tears thick on their faces. Duane, grunting and gasping, throws himself at Connie, can't quite get his footing on her lap there, so he falls back to the floor. Then he leaps at Kristy. Human laughing and crying are indistinguishable to Duane, but the intensity of what they are doing is frightening.

8

HEN THE VETERINARIAN returns that evening, Connie Creighton and Duane greet him down in the kitchen, and the good doctor makes a gentle, interested fuss over Duane. Then Connie says, "The big dog is upstairs."

And the vet looks her in the eyes in a polite pleasant way, but he does not laugh.

Upstairs in the hot apartment Kristy is sitting by the bed in the dim green-gold light, too dim a light for reading great novels or writing to a friend, a light made only for vigils, and she says quickly, "He's the same."

"No better, no worse, huh?" the vet says gently. He lowers his book satchels and now a fat gym bag onto the floor in front of the window seat and asks if there is better light.

Connie, standing at the door behind him, flips a switch. From overhead, four floodlights come to life. Light brighter than nature's noon.

The vet nods his appreciation to Connie. Unlike "human doctors," he doesn't ask the "ladies" to leave the room. He just empties syringes and bottles and various sealed items onto a sheet of examining paper on the window seat. "Outside your windows, it's just your treetops?"

"Paranoid?" Kristy taunts him. "Or are we thinking of Robert Drummond's modesty?"

The vet smiles. "Paranoid. Aren't you?"

Kristy laughs. "It's all treetops. And . . . yes, Woody, I'm scared."

Connie stays back by the door, arms folded under her big breasts, feet a little bit spaced, her top lip twitching slightly. She has not been hovering around the sick man like her daughter has.

The vet asks, "Is there a way to get the temperature of this room a little less hot? It must be more than eighty degrees. It's not healthy for even the healthy." He glances at both women. "But especially now for our friend who is very sick. We need to get that fever down. And even after his fever's down, a moderately warm room and a few blankets would be my advice."

While Kristy's chin goes up—not one to like taking orders, even gentle ones—the vet tugs the peach sheet away and deftly turns the gasping, groaning man onto his side. "I'm embarrassed to have been so taken by surprise earlier today that I didn't bring a thermometer. I'd like to have had Robert's temperature before so we could compare it with now. You know Robert is very sick."

"We know," says Kristy, narrowing one eye, chin still high. She grips a bedpost with one hand. Yes, hovering.

Connie has swept over to the thermostat and has given it a significant twist. Her skirt is long. A tiered print of small but bright impetuous fruits on black. Her big-necked sweater is black. Black downplays big breasts.

A thump downstairs means Duane is, against all odds now, still trying to enforce the laws of regularity . . . having hopped up onto the senator's bureau by way of shorter pieces of furniture . . . his head cocked, eyes on the ceiling. The senator's Yale graduation picture now lies facedown on the floor, but the glass is still whole. One needlepoint pillow is deflated, its loose rag stuffing tossed about like so many dead birds.

The vet finds Robert's rectal temperature to be 106°F. He asks if there's a floor lamp, which Connie briskly retrieves from the second floor. Soon the bag of clear fluid is hung from the lamp and the doctor is working an IV into Robert's left arm between the yellow ancient-faced sun and the Christmas tree.

And now blood. Two pints, Kristy's eyes widen on that crimson, that eternally vulgar, yet compelling crimson. She looks into the vet's eyes. He raises a brow, goes back to fussing with the tubes.

"How did you get that?" she asks breathlessly.

"Don't ask," he replies.

"You saw his blood type in his wallet."

"Let's drop the subject," he says with twinkling eyes. Then, "OK, nurse. Ready for instructions?" While the blood begins to work its way into the patient through a second IV, Woody shows Kristy how to check the IV for the clear fluids, which need to be administered "wide open" for the first hour, then adjusted. He explains that Robert is restless, will probably have the thing knocked out before long. Then, too, there's the possibility of seizures. Before he leaves he would like to tie Robert down . . . with sheets. Could she locate a few more flat sheets? And Kristy should keep a very close eye on him through the night. He presses into Kristy's hand large capsules sealed in foil. "Rectal suppositories. Every six hours. Until he can swallow." Kristy does not blush. But she *thinks* she blushes as he explains how deeply the suppositories must be inserted.

Meanwhile, the vet injects syringes of antibiotic into the IV. "If he comes to, get him to drink. A lot. Get him up. Get him to move around for short periods of time. Get him to drink a lot of water and . . ." He smiles. ". . . something I don't get to prescribe very often. Juices." He apologizes again and again for not having the best medicine has to offer the human race. He promises to come back in the morning. He asks Kristy if she would mind keeping a temperature chart and using . . . yes . . . the rectal thermometer.

"Whatever needs to be done to save his life," she replies in her professional voice, her women's studies department chair voice.

And then Connie's deep, almost manly voice, coming from the wicker rocker over by the rolltop desk, "To live only to die."

Kristy squares her shoulders, does not acknowledge this.

Connie persists, "In the electric chair, right?"

The vet looks across the bed at Kristy as he fusses some more with the IVs and floor lamp. Her little dark floofy cap of hair, two goldfish earrings. Long loose-sleeved silk shirt one might call Athena blue. And about thirty blue silk fabric-covered buttons. And her dark-lashed eyes, the same blue. Athena, yes. Such a long, lovely neck. A young thirty-one-year-old goddess. Immortal, and easily pissed off. A true temple of piping-hot feminist liberal empowerment. No need for teeth and claws, the 1990s system serves her well. And that way she moves her shoulders. Nothing like any of the vet assistants Dr. Kenneth Wood has ever worked with before.

Now Kristy reaches out and finds the stiffened areas on Robert's left hand, callous and thickened skin, bumpy scars, and deep musculature. The hand like the rest of him, 106°... almost too hot to hold. And when this hand tightens around hers—a sudden fierce grip—she gasps. The vet looks only as the hand goes lax again, but now Robert turns his head, left and right, back and forth, groaning. And Robert speaks. "They wan' you to stop. O... K?"

Kristy knows Robert is forty-four, but keeps picturing him to have a younger voice. Each time he has spoken today, it has surprised her. For Robert does not have anything like a young man's voice.

Connie has left the room, reappears with an armload of flat sheets, none white, all pastels—blue, lavender, and mint. The vet and Kristy work quietly to tie both Robert's arms firmly to the bed. And then another sheet around his waist.

Then there's the wait for the last blood pouch to empty. The vet sits some, stands some. He doesn't get into any conversation with Connie or Kristy. Indeed, he does seem to be shy, his confidence exclusive to his work of healing.

After he has packed up, he stands a moment watching Robert's slowly rising and falling chest. From chest to navel, hidden now in knotted sheets, not much hair, just a shadowy dark, slender ribbon. The vet rearranges the ice pillows, one across the chest and stomach. "I'll be back in the morning," he tells Connie as he passes her chair and she stands to show him out, but first he turns to glance back at the form on the bed, which he salutes, a real brisk, real military salute. Then heads out.

FTER CONNIE has gone to bed, Kristy goes into her own little living room and sinks into her big, soft two-cushion love seat and gives the remote control a squeeze. The news. She finally gives in to it.

And sure enough, "manhunt intensified," several pictures of Robert, including one composite drawing from witness descriptions. The newscaster explains fast and buoyantly that forty-four-year-old building contractor Robert Daniel Drummond had been " 'discouraged with the way things were going in this country,' " had specifically complained about " 'corporate socialist pigs in Congress,' " and with another man, now dead—his brother-in-law Kevan Libby—had organized the Snow Men, a small armed "antigovernment" militia. TV wide-angled cameras sweep across the Drummond home in Maine, a small frame house with a new shingled addition, a small modern barn, electric fence, cattle switching their tails, red-and-yellow splotched humpy mountain beyond the field, and in the foreground a single pine tree with a massive trunk with its arms raised as if in a rage.

A yellow snowplow blade, some oil drums, staging, hardwood skids, and stuff.

"In school," an elderly teacher recalls in a shrieky monotone, "he was not a good student. He could have been. But he never tried, not enough encouragement at home. His mind was always elsewhere. He was from a big family ... a *large* family. There was no encouragement that anyone could see."

Another teacher: "Bobby was quiet. You couldn't know him."

An old schoolmate: "I knew him well. He liked animals. He liked fixin' up rabbit hutches. And special trees for their chickens. He was tough. We all called him Ruff ... even his mum called him that ... Ruff."

Another schoolmate: "We always called him Ruff. You couldn't hurt him. Teachers tried. Principal tried. They did all sorts of things to him."

Another schoolmate: "I knew him real good. I still know him. I see him around. I remember two teachers ... they stood Ruff up in study hall, you know, told him to stand. They laughed about his smell. He smelled like cattle. Well, a lot of us had cattle t'home. But these teachers wanted us to especially notice Ruff's cow smell ... for some reason. He was always the one they went after. He was going with Paula Macy at the time ... He always had one. A girl. And he always had cigarettes. And an old car. I'm sure when he was out with Paula, he smelled like Old Spice. He always had a good-lookin' steady girl to keep him happy and a car to look after. And this makes teachers ugly, you know. You know. They just want you to study."

Another old schoolmate tells the reporter, "He liked

guns. He hunted a lot. And he liked guns. Back in those days nobody thought much of it. But nowadays, if you like guns, you're a weirdo or something. I guess he was! A weirdo!" Shakes her head. Looks sad.

Again the camera sweeps across the entrances of the Parker House in Boston, stops at a revolving door. Delicately and considerately—alluding to, but not actually speaking, the FCC-disapproved F-word—the newscaster's voice explains that just inside this revolving door, the Snow Men very quickly surrounded the senator, forced him to his knees, while Drummond screamed, "Clear out!! Clear those people out!! This fucker's gonna ricochet!!" and then putting a gun to the base of the senator's skull, spoke quietly, "Die, fucker, die." And fired twice, and one of the ricocheting bullets did, in fact, wound one of his own companions.

Now Kristy realizes that some of the blood on Robert's jeans and boots was probably the senator's.

She shuts the TV off. Sits in the near dark, the curtainless dormer windows gloating pinkish from the security lighting outside. She stares at the blue-lighted digitals of her microwave in her kitchenette beyond the door, flickering to the next minute.

Die, Robert Drummond, die.

10

SHE SLEEPS AWHILE in this chair, sitting up, head back. She is awakened by her own snore, which happens now and then when sitting up sleeping on planes, and it is so embarrassing. She can't imagine getting up and going into her own bedroom and getting undressed. Even if there were no possibility of seizures and ripped-out IV, even if it weren't for melting ice that needed continuous replacement. She feels disgusted with her mother's sense of humor about this, her staginess. And Art. If only Art had been more practical, less... less emotional. Less willful. Less principled. Possessed less integrity. If only ...

She stands up and goes into the study room and sees the red flashes over by the farthest dormer that mean there are messages piling up on her phone ... and maybe a fax or two. And she sees that Robert has flung one leg off the edge of the bed, his toes touching the floor. And the peach sheet is still lying over a chair where the vet had tossed it. And she sees that by her slim watch it's about time to adjust the IV, and time for the temperature taking, and the suppositories.

Her heart thuds. Her face and jaws begin to ache. She goes over to the bed and she sees that the IV is still in place. Looks good to her, still inserted slantwise in the vein under clear tape. She makes the needed adjustment for the next 250 cc's. She sees that his breathing is easier. No more gasping, though he still breathes through his open mouth. She swallows. Her throat dry. Head pounding. *Leave him. Let him die. He's a monster.* She spreads an open hand on his shoulder. Still hot as hell. She loosens the sheets that bind him down. She looks over at the suppositories, the gloves, the paper with lines the vet made up to keep the temperatures and times recorded. She looks at the leg hanging off the bed. The room is still hot. She looks at the thermostat. It's turned all the way down. She doesn't want to open a window in this room, fearing a draft on him. So she goes into the little living room and raises one dormer window there. But the heat of two lower floors will always yearn up and gather.

She steps close into the reek of iodine and cigarettes, no gloves. She is bare-handed, the opulence of all feeling simmering on her palms and the tips of her fingers; she grips the dangling leg, swings it up onto the bed, and flips him onto his side and squinting first at the thermometer, and then to where she'll drive it into him, she says mischievously, "This is a dog thermometer, Ruff."

And when it is done—even the suppository, which she does with bare fingers, feeling the heat of his rectum with one hand, hotter than the heat of his hip, which she grips with the other, then easing him back again into his nest of ice—she sees that his eyes are open, eyes that seem a darker brown in this green-gold stained-glass light, and he grimaces and says, "Jesus Christ," and reaches toward his damaged shoulder with his left hand and then drops that hand across his ribs and explains in a matter-of-fact voice, "It's bitin' me. Get it off." And his eyes are leaden, fixed on the lamp.

She walks to her kitchenette and washes her hands in the sink, doing everything wrong. She knows this. Her mind and heart are trotting down a very wrong little path here. She hangs her head a moment, forearms on the sink. In this prayerful pose, her long neck is its loveliest, the little ducktail of dark hair at the nape. In this prayerful pose, she has negated all she has played hard for, the prize being the right to stand erect and answer to no one, to be complete, to be an entity, created in the image of... of... of... What?

She is nothing like her mother. Not even to look at. She is only moderately busty, not the great quaking tits that Connie has. Kristy's build is her father's, willowy and self-possessed. Self-possessed? No, self-contained. No, how about self-conscious? She feels her "self" has been shredded like a cloud and dispersed over the last half of her life. She sees herself as flat as a faxed message. She sees herself as a 4.0 grade average. A gold seal. Valedictorian. A glowing introduction. A forty-five-minute talk before blank droopy-eyed faces. Friendly applause. The stub of another plane flight. A restaurant place mat. Her name. Her fine strong maiden name, which is no longer called a maiden name. And there's no such thing as a married name. How far we've come from the Jesus of Nazareth days. But see there, the glowing introduction. Kristy of Radcliffe. Kristy of the long chain of great institutional honors. She, in this prayerful pose tonight, whispers, "Help me, God."

She returns to the bedside, and his eyes are still open and still leaden. He swallows. He coughs. Jerks his whole body in restlessness. Tries to turn onto his side, drawing his knees up, then flops back onto his back, IV tube straining, bags of ice crunching. Then he settles down. She turns away. She marks his temperature on the chart: 105°F under where the vet had written 106°F. She whispers, "You're getting better, my darling."

And behind her back, he laughs, then says thickly, "You can have the whole...thing. That's allll riiiii..." Now she ties the pastel sheets around his waist and forearms again, snug but not tight, the way the doctor showed her. Then she reaches to put on another soft light, a white silk-shaded lamp in the next dormer, that dormer having a window seat, too, and bookshelves, a few stuffed animals on the seat, somewhat brutalized by baby Kristy, a person she no longer knows but has been told by experts is important to relocate. Where is baby Kristy? Where will baby Kristy take Professor Kristy? Up or down?

And she brushes a few stuffed animals to one side and heaves the window open. WIDE. And the cold night air slithers in like a live thing, reptilish and dry.

She returns to the bed and sees he has raised his right knee again and his eyes are still open. She reaches and combs his hair a little with her fingers, hair thinning at the temples. Forehead and skull sweating, sticky as Scotch tape. His mouth is closed. He swallows. He stares now at the other lamp, the light of it reflected on the slanted ceiling. And she keeps stroking his hair. And she asks, "Where are you, Ruff?"

His voice vibrates in his neck. But he doesn't open his mouth. He looks at her. He smiles. A blank-eyed, close-mouthed smile. A smile that means nothing.

With her knuckles she neatens his big mustache.

He coughs. Once.

She looks at the swastika, a soft faded blue. She sighs.

She sees something move in the corner of her eye. His penis.

"Uh-huh," she says, grabs the plaid shirt from the post, drops it over him there. The room is starting to cool. Good. She'll consider the sheet and a blanket for him soon. She goes back to her love seat in the next room, waiting, listening to how nice and quiet he is now. She smokes a joint. She thinks about Pennsylvania. All of it. The department, the meetings, the faculty, her students, her friends there, her four million warnings for speeding, her dissertation, her apartment with almost no windows, the weather there, which is different.

11

SHE IS WAKENED by a rustling and a dream of hatching eggs, with dark things coming out of the eggs, like baby turtles, but not. It is a frightening dream and she wakes with a cry. And she sees him standing there in the one open French door to the study room, morning light pouring in on the rugs behind him and on one shoulder of the plaid shirt that he wears, unbuttoned, his right arm hanging at his side, his left hand gripping the door frame. No pants. There's the dark hair and the long uncircumcised penis that shivers as he takes another step toward her. His eyes on her are wide awake. His face feverflushed. He says, "Where's my stuff?"

She jumps to her feet. She is tall, as tall as he, given the extra heel of her cowboy boots. She is not afraid. She understands he has untied himself and pulled the IV out. She understands he is wanting to move on, back out to the street . . . and the electric chair . . . or to eliminate more senators first.

She crosses her arms defiantly. "Aren't you going to ask, 'Where am I?' first?" She smiles.

"I know where I am."

This chills her.

He takes another step. But not a steady step. His legs shake. Like a hundred-year-old man. But his eyes are ever so lucid. On her face. Waiting for her to answer his question.

But still smiling, she asks, "So where *are* you?"

"Boston. Beantown. Home of the Red Sox."

She laughs, a low, lovely bray. Then she moves without hesitation toward him, then to the side of him, through the doorway, her hip brushing him. She heads for the window seat filled with light and the flutterings of jays in the spruces, the swaying shadow of the empty and rotting little feeder she hung out there one fall when she had spent another "healing time" here a few years ago. The varnished wood of the window seat glows yellow gold and glossy. The room is cold now. But a nice cold. Fresh. The sound of morning traffic coming from the open dormer window beyond the computer and desk.

She picks up his knife and wallet, his belt and gun shells. He is still back at the doorway. Gripping the door frame with his left hand but now turned to face her. With no pants, just the unbuttoned shirt, she is so reminded of a young child, and then another image flashes into her head of the two teachers making Robert stand before the class in study hall—in some sense naked—hearing them critique in scholarly tones his smell.

She tosses the belt and knife and wallet onto the bed. The gun cartridges she's a bit tender with. Lines them up nice, like little toy cars. And then she sees that between the leaking ice pillows, he has wet the bed. Or maybe it's just the yellow of his laborious sweating. She looks over at him again, looks him up and down, but not as his teachers had, with scorn, not as the FBI will soon do, with infinite and righteous hatred, but with softness, a softness that this edgy, angry, rivalrous ultrafeminist, Ms. Kristina Creighton, has never shown in her adult life toward any man.

She says, "Your clothing was bloody. The doctor suggested it be burned. I presume in case of AIDS."

He screws up his face with disgust. "AIDS?"

Unless the murdered senator had AIDS, she figures that that complication is now ruled out. And she recalls that Senator Kip Davies was especially eloquent on why people who got AIDS deserved it and how clean needles or AIDS research or free distribution of condoms was "outrageous."

Oh, Senator Davies! Let us recall him as he lived and breathed. Senator Davies was the most flamboyantly outspoken congressman speaking against constitutional rights to gays. Meanwhile, "We will put a stop to bloody babies in wastebaskets" and "America is tired of all those welfare queens with bleached hair and a can of beer, wearing hot pants, riding the streets of America in their Caddies!" and "We have a proud heritage of firearms. No criminal is going to get far climbing into an armed American's bedroom window!" and "We are tired of these foreign herds taking our jobs!" and "Every time a flag is burned, I feel the rage of the very fathers who gave us the country that that flag stands for!"

But the record shows Davies voted for several antigun measures and was proabortion! And was in the men's room or something when the flag desecration bill was voted on ... or out writing his best-seller book on his life as a patriot.

Davies never seemed to quite get the hang of it, how you can fleece the people in a whirl of dizzying complexities and myths and age-old PR, how you can convince the public that "toxic waste is good for you," that giant gobs of money in giveaways and tax breaks and sweetheart deals to corporations and more investor protections mean jobs. You don't have to say whose jobs. You don't have to say good jobs. Just "jobs." That the rising GDP means the floating of all boats, if not today, soon! That making millions of welfare moms work means more jobs for others! That prison labor is actually the "Volunteers of America." That since more people murder other people in states where they have the death penalty, this means the death penalty works. That marijuana makes people into psychos and must be stopped with conspiracy laws, "drug exceptions to the Bill of Rights," lots of warrantless searches and seizures and neighbors spying on each other, army guns held to little kids' heads while SWAT teams stand on their parents' faces and tear the plaster out of the bedroom walls, and more cops with dogs to search schools while prisons fill to the max with nice people and helicopters cause pictures to fall off the walls. "This is hard for America, but drugs are harder. Oh ... well, yuh, maybe marijuana doesn't turn 'em into psychopathic killers ... but good people do not smoke marijuana. Marijuana is ... you know, low. It just isn't good for you. It could cause something unhealthy. And we want you all healthy. We care."

Senator Kip Davies just couldn't get the hang of these read-my-lips doublespeak doublethink gymnastics.

Senator Davies's lies had a more blunderishness to them. And yet he had gotten away with it for six terms.

The only people he made visibly mad were the "liberals." The lesser of the two evils for the redneck Republicans back home? Was there really *worse?*

Yes, Davies had gotten away with it. Until Robert Drummond and his militia, Robert Drummond with the GOP tattoo and the swastika. Something's fishy here. Why, Robert Drummond, why?

Now here in the home of yet another senator, Robert Drummond stands with an expression of vague disgust. And Kristy Creighton tells him, "I'll shop for some new clothes for you. Right away. Tell me your size and what you like—"

"Not plaid," he says with even deeper disgust. "And not pink." He squints at the sleeve of his dangling arm. Now he starts to take a step into the study room, sways really badly, raises his left hand to his eyes. She rushes over to him, wraps her arm around his back and chest, and walks with him. "The doctor said you need rest. I'll change your bed." She steers him to the low wicker chair her mother had sat in last evening. He goes down rather heavily. It crackles under his weight.

She heaps his belt, wallet, jackknife, and cartridges into his left hand and "lap." His right arm hangs out over the chair arm, fingers open.

While she changes the bed, he watches her with his frighteningly perceptive-looking dark eyes, maybe just seeming so perceptive because he had been so "unperceptive" for so long.

She keeps expecting him to ask, *Who are you?,* but he doesn't. He asks no questions.

She tells him, "The doctor is coming back. Soon. And my mother. I'm surprised she hasn't already been up. I think she's having . . . concerns. Harboring a fugitive is not the same as a parking ticket."

He looks at his wallet but doesn't open it.

When she's done with the bed and cries out a cheery "Voilà" and throws out a hand as if it were not a bed but a rabbit pulled from a hat, he says, "Thank you," in a warm way, nodding his head once on the word thank.

She helps him to the bed and he slumps there on the edge of it, looking out at the trees and the sky, which is roaring with the takeoff of a jet from Logan very nearby. She goes to her refrigerator and pours him a tall glass of water. "Poland Spring," she says thrillingly, holding it out to him. "From Maine."

He looks steadily into her eyes and one brow flickers knowingly. "You looked in my wallet."

She laughs. "Well, yes, I did. But, Ruff, you're famous! I didn't have to look in your wallet to recognize you." Then she realizes he was teasing, one of those teasing thinks-she's-stupid kind of guys she so despises.

He drinks the cold water. Deeply. Drinks it all.

"More?"

"Sure."

When she returns and places it in his hand, he says, "Thank you," again, warmly, explaining how very thirsty he is, and his voice is thick, a nice thick-necked rich voice and his accent is western Maine, the mountains . . . almost like the comedians who make fun . . . but different, not strained . . . not stretched out flat . . . just easy and artless and unaffected . . . like the jays outside the window there screaming and gossiping in the voices they hatched out with.

She reaches and feels his forehead. He lets her. She realizes how proprietorial she has become of him, as if his temperature were her own, his skin her skin, his space her space. His forehead is still alarmingly hot.

"How do you feel?" she asks.

"Shitty."

"Well, you should have seen how you felt yesterday. I can't believe you are alive."

He shrugs, then winces. Looks down at his dangling right hand.

She is thinking it is time to mark his temperature with the rectal thermometer. Unh-uh. This is where she draws the line.

He says in a low voice, "Where's my revolver?"

She lies quickly. "My friend has it. When you're all better, we'll give it back."

He looks up at her hands, wringing slightly. He says, "Yep. Fine. Don't matter really." He looks back out the window. Then he frowns and looks at her again. "Would you do me a favor?"

She nods. Fast and childlike.

"'Twas a bitch gettin' this shirt on. I need it off. You could maybe help me make a sling or somethin' with it. If I take the weight off this shoulder it helps." He leans forward, sets the water glass on one of the straight-back chairs, winces again, then drops his hand onto his bare left thigh. Something deft and quite cool about that hand. Capable. So he's left-handed. Fortunate in misfortune.

"Let me find something else for a sling. Without your shirt, you'll be cold."

He casts his eyes sideways at her, almost a flirt thing. "I'm from Maine, remember?"

She smiles, goes to him, starts to tug the shirt down

over the bandaged side first. He winces and groans. Not a silent sufferer? Once the shirt is off, he suggests making this into a sling, to tie the sleeves around his neck. Of course! What other way would you make a sling? But Kristy plays along. Her eyes, as ever, are drawn to the colorific pageantry of his arms.

"Don't look at that shit. 'Twas kid stuff," he says.

"Even GOP?"

He looks at her levelly. "No."

"Maybe you mean the swastika."

"I made that myself in sixth grade. We all did 'em. Wrote 'em on books, on desks. Weren't no Jews around. It had nothin' to do with that. It was just fun to do . . . fun to draw 'em . . . and the teachers would go berserk."

"You liked that. Torturing teachers?"

He sneers, no words necessary. He coughs now. A very deep smoker's cough. Covers his mouth politely. Winces in pain with each hard heave of the shoulders. Presses the knuckles of his good hand to the left side of his groin.

"I've heard that tattoos can be removed. You could get that one removed."

"Nah," he says. "I don't give a shit."

"But it's awful."

"I don't know any Jews. They ain't goin' to see it."

"But a person doesn't have to be Jewish to find it offensive."

" 'Tain't offensive. It's just a thing."

"Suit yourself."

She fits his arm into the center of the plaid fabric, then lifting, ties the sleeves in a knot at the nape of his neck, feeling the furnacelike heat of his skin, and then sees he is plastered with goose bumps. She considers other shirts in her closet . . . or something of her father's. "Let me get one of those blankets over you. Make you cozy."

Cold or not, she's having a real problem with the shaking of his loose penis each time he shifts his weight there on the edge of the bed. It's worse for her now than when he was in deep, fevered sleep. He had been more of a gasping Michelangelesque sculpture, a partial Pietà in rainbow colors. High art. Sort of. But now, she's never been so horny. Maybe it's the tattoos, too. All of it. The whole Robert/Ruff package. Everything about him speaks to her glands.

He asks, "You wouldn't have a cigarette, would you?"

"Not in this house. This is a smoke-free residence," she says with finality. She reaches for a blanket. "Well, not smoke free." She shakes out the blanket.

She helps him get situated under a fresh sheet, then tosses on the blanket, heads to her kitchenette to fetch him a little something. When she returns, he is on his side, deep in the covers, blanket all the way up to his neck. His teeth are chattering violently.

"Oh, I'm sorry," she says, squatting by the bed, looking into his face.

"It goes back and forth," he says miserably. "First cookin', then freezin'."

"The doctor will be here any minute." She lowers her voice to a whisper. "You like grass?"

"Yep."

"I wasn't sure. Being militia . . . I . . . thought grass might be a little too left-wing for you."

He laughs. A happy laugh. And runs the fingers of his good hand down over his face. "What about your mum?"

"She doesn't care. As long as we are discreet."

He chuckles into the pillow. "What a mother!"

"I'm not sure about the vet, though. So maybe we better wait."

"Vet?"

She flushes. "The doctor . . . the best we could do. Under the circumstances."

Robert blinks his bleary eyes a bunch of times fast. He chuckles. "Neat."

12

DOWN IN THE BIG ELL kitchen of open dark beams, a fireplace with four cast-iron hatches for baking beans and biscuits, authentic wallpaper and almost-authentic light fixtures, but also modern gadgets and appliances, of course, and then a broad slate sink set in mauve-and-white and blue-and-white tiles with sun splayed over them in a brightness that's a bit blinding . . . through this marvel kitchen Connie Creighton hurries to and fro. Connie Creighton still in a black sweater, but a different black sweater, and now jeans and sneakers and your standard red bandanna tied around her tight bun of frizzy sandy hair (her hanging-around-the-house look).

Duane stands in the middle of the floor with his head cocked, listening to the whole house, his small feet wide apart, braced.

Connie makes calls, canceling all her appointments for the day. She tosses her pen toward the pen vase from a good distance, and it makes its mark with a clunk! She howls, "The *Globe*! The *Globe*! Oh, where is the *Globe*?!" And pops in and out of doors, wearing her Colonial-style reading glasses, flipping through reference books. Duane keeps racing over to the door that is closed, the one across from the dining-room door that leads to the back stairs going up. He hangs around the pantry way, sniffing, grumbling to himself. Connie starts something fruity in the blender, forgets about it, puts a cup of water in the microwave, goes off to put on the TV, doesn't see what she wants, leaves it talking to itself, dashes into the library again to come out with yet another two reference books, one under each arm. One is a medical text. She is, all the while, dashing around Priss, the housekeeper Priss who is not usually kept in the dark about much.

Priss narrows her eyes. Priss has her very yellow curls up in a red bandanna just like Connie's. Priss never wears black to minimize. Her tight T-shirt is purple. She is a fortyish gal as busty as Connie, but big and shaky in the middle, too, with a tiny rear and stick thighs. Connie's rear and legs are neither sticks nor vast, but she'd rather be without the slight saddlebag effect. But hell, aerobics are dull. As Connie heads back into the "cozy room" (the smaller parlor) and flicks through channels violently, carrying the remote out to the kitchen in her mouth, while flipping through the most recent L.L.Bean catalog, Priss speaks. "What. Is. Going. On?"

And Connie, just realizing where the remote control is, tosses it on the little antique table, sputtering out the taste of plastic. "Ohhhhhhhh," waves a hand to dismiss the notion of something going on. Thumbs again through the catalog. Tosses it. Sighs. Stares at the humming refrigerator, her reading glasses at the ends of her fingers.

"Connie," Priss insists.

Connie looks at Priss. Tosses her glasses on the table

with the remote control, takes a deep breath, throws out her chest, raises her face, raises a hand to the heavens (or ceiling, however you want to take it), indicating, yes, something beyond the ceiling . . . something. And replies at last in her most guttural and booming voice, with a kind of Richard Burton accent: " 'The quality of mercy . . . is not strainnnn'd. It droppeth as the gentle rainnnn from heaven . . . Upon the place beneath: it is twice blessss'd; It blesseth herrrrr that gives and himmmmmmmm that takes: 'Tis mightiest in the mightiest: it becommmmmmmmz the throned monarch better than his crown!' " And then closing her eyes and dropping her head, takes a single step forward, the loose, sandy ringlets around her ears flopping. She throws up her head, eyes wide, makes a sweeping gesture toward the back pantry door, and booms hoarsely, " '*Annnnnd earthly power doth then showwww likest God's Whennnnn mercy seasons justice!*' "

And then the buzzer buzzes over the pantry-way door, meaning someone is at the gates.

THE VET ARRIVES on the third floor with Connie; Connie holds Duane. Art arrives a moment later. Art had been detained a little in the kitchen by Priss, who told him Connie is acting more bizarre than usual. After lunch a little paid vacation will begin for Priss until "the problem" is resolved. But for now, Priss is downstairs noticing things.

The vet doesn't explode with joy to see that Robert is raised up on one elbow, Robert looking him square in the face with that too-perceptive expression. The vet just smiles a closed-lip smile and says, "Hello, Robert."

But with Connie, it's a smile. All her perfect creamy teeth. And she speaks as if to an audience in a much larger room, an auditorium perhaps. "Allouishis! Magic happens!"

And Art says, "I prayed."

Connie looks at him skeptically.

Art flushes.

The man in the bed, sitting up now, brown blanket piled around his hips and the sun now licking his colorific left arm and gleaming on the remaining bit of liquid in the disconnected IV pouch, looks at Art a long moment and says clearly, "I thank you."

And Art laughs. "Anytime. Anytime."

This is not Connie's first visit upstairs this morning. She and her daughter have had a bit of conferencing in Kristy's kitchenette nearly twenty minutes ago, but Robert had been very quiet then, very buried in blankets, and Connie hadn't experienced that glittery steady look of his eyes. She settles now into the wicker chair and strokes Duane, who tries to slip from her grip. His job has gotten even more vast now than he previously imagined. His eyes gaze around the room, memorizing, filing. He sniffs the air in every direction.

The vet stands over the temperature chart, deep in thought. Art backs all the way up to Connie's chair and without looking at her asks in a low voice, "When will the senator be home for that dinner gig?"

Connie speaks gravely, "He is expected a week from Thursday."

"You going to tell him?"

"Jehovah in the heavens! No!"

As he slips the plaid sling off Robert's neck, the vet asks, "You been up at all, Robert?"

Robert says, "Yep."

A stethoscope swings out from the vet's hands. He warms it a moment in his fingers, then fitting it to his ears, presses it to different areas of Robert's back. "Breathe deeply."

Robert obeys.

Vet inquires, "You a smoker?"

Robert murmurs, "Yep."

Vet makes no comment about cigarettes. Not even a tsk. He steps around Robert's shoulder and now listening to the chest finds the heart. Then again lungs. "Breathe deep."

Robert obeys. Then, "You can't get kitties and doggies to do that, can you?" he says as the vet turns away to lay the instrument upon one of his satchels.

The vet turns back, smiling, pats Robert's shoulder.

"Grrrrrrroof!" Robert pretends to bite the hand.

Everybody thinks this is pretty funny. At this moment, everybody kind of loves Robert.

Duane is alert. He is especially watching Robert, whose behavior is suspicious, Duane thinks.

The vet peels off the bandages. The wound is horrible to look at. The bullet, having entered from the back of his thick shoulder, has made quite a jellyish mess of the front. The vet says, "Robert, tell me. What can you do with your hand?"

"I can't close it. I can open it . . . like this . . . but I can't close it."

Vet says, "And you have feeling in your hand and fingers, right?"

"Ye . . . p." He speaks this slowly, as if not really sure.

"Going to apply some cold, a bit smarting ointment. Your infection could still do you in if we aren't diligent. I'll leave some of this for you . . . enough for the week."

Robert closes his eyes as if pain won't come if you don't look at it. He winces as the ointment goes on, looks through squinted eyes at Connie and the dog.

Connie looks back at him, kind of thumps one of her sneakered feet.

Kristy watches closely wherever the vet puts his hands

on Robert, whenever he picks up another sterile wipette or cotton swab.

Vet says, "Robert. Tell me. When was your last tetanus shot?"

Robert says he doesn't remember. Fifteen, twenty years, maybe.

The vet sighs, noticeable disappointment. Then presses and prods the shoulder a bit, Robert wincing, drawing his knees up reflexively under the blanket. Vet says, "A lot of swelling. Without X rays, I can't tell you whether it's bone chips, tendons ... or something else. You really need a neurosurgeon to go in there."

He disengages all the trappings of the IV. He gives Robert several injections. Without looking up, he asks Kristy, who is hovering, "How did the suppositories work out? Did you need them ... or had he stepped out of the fog by then?"

Kristy answers without a hitch, "They worked out well."

The vet looks down again at the temperature chart.

Robert is looking at Kristy perceptively.

The vet says, "Well, you can use your oral thermometer now. And I have one here"you can have in case you can't find your own, as often happens in households." He peels the crisp paper off, slips the thermometer into Robert's mouth under the coarse business of the mustache.

Robert is looking at Kristy, a hard, meaningful gaze, even though with a thermometer in one's mouth, one can look kind of silly.

When the vet reads the thermometer, he marks it on the chart with care, his handwriting tiny.

Kristy asks, "What is it?"

"Hundred and three."

"Eayehh." She looks at Robert. "You don't feel good, do you?"

Robert makes an ever-so-slight suggestion of a head shake, curls his top lip a bit, looks down at the vet's hands as they probe around for another place to jam another needle into. As the needle slips in, the vet apologizes again. "I wish I could do more... for your shoulder. I'm really sorry." He makes a gently desperate, hopeless face, shakes his head.

Robert grunts. "Don't matter anyway."

The vet tells Art to tell Mark to come around his office at noon, to ask to speak to him personally and he'll have some oral antibiotic and iron pills for Robert. He promises to visit again tonight, tells Kristy to keep up the temperature chart.

And then looking down at his own hands as shy people are known to do, he says, "To operate on a human being... it takes an anesthesiologist, which we do not have... and you'd want a qualified neurosurgeon for this, not me. The loss of a hand is more... to think about than the loss of a paw."

He reaches for Robert's good left hand and Robert's fingers close on his. The healthy squeeze of a good hand, the miracle journey of synapses from brain to fingers. Great medicine, great cathedrals, cozy homes, food, all made possible by this quick ecstatic journey. And killing? He looks from Robert's hand to Robert's eyes. Yeah, the killer's hand. War. The world and its multitudinous hands, each knows its errand.

After he is gone and Connie has gone down to show

him out and Kristy has gone to shower and change out of yesterday's clothes, Art steps up to the bed, with Robert quietly stretched out on his side again, blanket up to his ears. Art puts out his hand. Robert sees with weary feverish eyes the uniform shoulder patch of his militia in Art's hand. The abominable snowman with its terrible grinning face, standing, legs spread on the summit of a silhouetted mountaintop. Art tells him, "I spared it." He presses it into Robert's hand.

Robert says, "Thank you," warmly, and draws the patch in under the blankets and stares out at Art in a way that looks like he might fade again into that leaden, unseeing, bad-feeling, dark hot place he had just come from a few hours ago.

PRISS, NOT ON HER surprise paid vacation yet, though she now knows about it. Priss, happy about her impending surprise vacation but who is made even more wildly suspicious that something really weird is up. Priss, bustling down the back stairs and into the center hall with two duffel bags of laundry bumping and fishtailing along the orangy pine floor behind her. Priss sees a movement. She sees that it is Connie standing in the front entryway, just standing there, a hand on the back of her neck like she's just been stung by a bee. And Duane at her feet, staring up at her hand.

"Is everything OK with the senator?" Priss asks, having heard the phone a moment ago.

Connie jumps, startled. Hadn't she heard Priss clombering toward her?

Priss says, "Connie, is the senator OK?"

Connie is now tapping her closed lips with a knuckle, a calculating look. "Ah . . . no . . . yes . . . just a friend."

But really it was the FBI planning to send a couple of guys to protect Connie and Kristy here and to tag along when either of the two women needs to go out. They think for some reason Robert Drummond might still be in the city and they fear that Connie and Kristy might be targets of Drummond's next move. She looks down into Duane's bright eyes. She told the FBI fellow that she is an artist and needs her privacy. She told him forcefully. She told him with just a tiny hint of her Joe Friday impersonation, with just a teeny twinge of Humphrey Bogart. Connie isn't really scared yet. Not yet. She still has a foot in that sunny place of her above-the-law influentiality. Yep, the FBI guy had backed off. For the time being. And now Priss. She finds it hard to look in Priss's face. Priss will be harder to fool than the government.

Priss gives the duffel bags several taming jerks of their drawstrings, pulling them up snug with her legs. "I hope everything's OK with everyone, Connie. It's pretty creepy out there, you know."

"Oh, yes. Everyone's OK. Just run ragged, as the saying goes. Too many irons in the fire."

Connie gives Priss's thick soft shoulder a squeeze and whirls away, Duane at her heels. She knows she will need to cancel another day's worth of activities. Fine. She'll get more done on the koala paintings. Fine. Fine. Fine. She strides into the big sunporch, which is her studio, and Duane races ahead, trying to predict which seat she wants so he can beat her to it. He guesses the big rocker, which is painted eggnog yellow with its deep print cushion. He lands up in it with such gusto, the back of it strikes the windowsill.

But Connie doesn't sit. She stands twisting one of the long ends of her knotted bandanna. And she stares at the middle of the long table of pencils and tubes of paint.

She is thinking about Congress, and the president and that lot. She is thinking how Jerry broke it to her, about how in the last vote the Senate took on the amended so-called "antiterrorism" bill—which called for increased uses of the death penalty for nonviolent so-called "acts of terror," in fact, mandatory death—he had voted yes. Mandatory. In other words, it will not be in the judge's hands. The decision for death, the premeditated deaths of real people, was decided by Jerry.

Like the mandatory life sentence for so many marijuana-related crimes, like all the union-busting schemes and government property giveaways and investor rights acts, Jerry had not seemed ashamed. He told her, "It is the climate." And he said it was "political necessity."

And she and he were walking on a beach, and she remembers she had her sunglasses in her hand so her eyes were very readable, and she looked at him and said coldly, "You mean it was the practical thing to do."

And he said by rote—like some people say things like *an eye for an eye* or *three sheets to the wind*—"It's a tough time. The climate is tough."

Connie knows. She knows the sound of Congress in session, the sound of a great energetic, well-lighted, rustling, mumbling space, their barks. And their smells. The smell that is nothing like a bunch of mule traders and poultry vendors and fishmongers and slave auctioneers and waddling, loaded-down mercenary scalpers, therefore you'd never think of a bunch of mule traders and poultry vendors and fishmongers and slave auctioneers and waddling, loaded-down mercenary scalpers, but see there!— the next deal going down, the sheer power of the handshake to move millions of lives out of one plane of existence to another.

Connie has heard more than one criminal lawyer say, It has nothing to do with guilt or innocence, but how you play the court and how motivated you are to play it.

Congress.

Courts.

Schools.

Human Services.

Prisons.

Taxes.

Death.

Grind. Chunk-chunk! Bing!

Connie knows the secret tendernesses of Jerry Creighton, the hurried but truly decent gestures to family and friends, the thinness of his time. His chronic headaches. His fears. His once-youthful dreams. He is not a terrible man. And yet, what is on his hands? Terror. Cruelty. Death. Weary relentless toil of a degraded population, ordinary lives played like pretty marbles for big business.

At an artists' colony where Connie worked on the illustrations for one of her earlier books, she remembers a composer who had come to breakfast once with a gleam in her dark eyes, her hair greasy from days and days of bringing music down from thin air . . . the deep chords of evil. For her piece was about evil. And she asked the others at the table, including Connie, how they would describe "evil." "Exactly what is 'evil'?" she wondered. Popovers were munched. Orange juice was gulped. Coffee stirred. No one was quick to answer. Though one poet finally chirped, "There's no such thing as evil really."

And everyone had cast their eyes upon her, all faces twisted sourly.

The composer looked into her untouched gray oatmeal, deeeep into it, her eyes seeing perhaps the opened hands and broken backs and prayerful faces of a few millennia. "Yes, evil exists. It has been coming to me as I work . . . its essence."

Connie cannot remember her own answer. But she knows it was different then than how she would describe evil these last ten years.

15

N EXT DAY, unseasonably warm for October, according to all the meteorologists, although as all of us in New England know, there's no such thing as unseasonable here. Almost all the windows are open in the Creighton home. Through the boiling busy purple-and-ivory sky, dark birds swing 'round in arcs. A thickness of warm rain on the way. And jets. All the usual low jets, heavy jets burning along slowly over the neighborhood.

Duane hates jets. He reports on jets by yapping around and around the rooms, throwing himself at windowsills, and believes these actions are what keep jets from landing inside this house.

Kristy is backing her Porsche out of the narrow bricked-over driveway, through the gates left wide open this morning for some expected deliveries of supplies Art has ordered, though Art is nowhere around yet. Late as usual. He's been late for work every day for forty years. Kristy is headed off to do some shopping.

When Connie appears in the third-floor study room, Duane charges ahead and lands on the bed, kissing

Robert's face. Kissing, kissing, kissing. "Ho ho ho," says Robert with a laugh, pushing away the kisses one-handedly, and he sits up. It is too hot for a blanket. He has just a nice flowery sheet. He had been sleeping. It's easy to tell. His plaid sling bunched on a chair. And his face pink and mashed on one side from the pillow.

Connie pulls up a chair in a managerial way. She has no kerchief in her hair today, just her sandy bun with a lot of loose frizziness and ringlets around her ears. A flowing summery dress of browns and greens. This is attractive. She is very attractive at times, other times unattractive, depending on her expression and mood. Her pale eyebrows are a little bushy, but her face is handsome, heart shaped, mouth a pale natural pink. Her daughter's brunette looks come from the senator. Connie is not a lot older than Robert, and this is clear in the air between them, like the static that makes her frizzy ringlets hop around.

Robert lets Duane lick his semiparalyzed hand. "Cute little guy," says Robert. "Cute Scottie."

"He's a cairn terrier," Connie corrects him gently.

With his good hand, Robert scratches Duane around the neck. Duane looks into Robert's brown eyes with his own brown eyes.

Connie asks, "Do you have a dog?"

"No house pets. Wife's allergic to dander."

"Oh. And what's your wife's name?"

"Cindy Mindy Squindy," he says quickly, and he looks serious.

Connie squints. "Is that her real name?"

He grins. "No. Her name is Cindy Drummond."

"Why, of course."

Duane can't get enough of licking Robert's loose

hand. Robert seems very patient. What Duane really wants is to check the Wound. He needs to win Robert's trust before he attempts this larger calling.

"What is Cindy Drummond like?"

"Nice."

"Nice?"

"Yes."

"What are the nicest things about her?" She asks this in a voice one uses on people of inferior intelligence, tries to check herself, but too late.

He seems not to notice. "She's a great mum. The best. She's good at everything. A genius lady." He looks down at Duane licking his wrist. He looks back at Connie. "She sews good. An' she does knittin'... sweaters, gloves, caps... even blankets. Knitted these blankets with big animals. And braided once a rug... all her sister's favorite colors. 'Twas for her sister."

He squints off into space over Connie's head. Connie watches him, fascinated. She sees the hard lines around his mouth that make parentheses around his mustache. She is spellbound with the little shrug of his shoulders as he works her question through his mind. And his voice, a little raspy from age and from god knows how many years of cigarettes.

"She always gets things goin' for surprise anniversaries... and, you know, the reunion thing... and food for after funerals. She's good at that." He wags his head a little, like to music. "She likes the phone. Yak yak yak ..." He trails off, then looks at Connie square on. "She used to garden with me an' Ma back at the other house. And she canned everything... even the weeds. An' ... slides. You know, sunsets... pictures of us campin' ... when we used to do that. An' pictures of everything ... for the slides ... and we all set around Christmas an' look at 'em an' eat pie an' the kids like to see themselves being stars. We never got video. She got into albums for a while ... but it got expensive. Friggin' price of pictures shot off to the moon." He looks at the farthest window, open with street sounds beyond. Frowns. "She does house bills. I do the business." He looks down at his useless right hand and Duane licking his forearm fiercely. "She used ta ... could go out all day long no matter how hot and pick a fuckin' shitloada blueberries and bake blueberry pies and blueberry biscuits for three solid days, an' stayin' up half the night ... but now she works ... so she don't do blueberries anymore. She always used to help me with hayin' and mendin' fences ... too busy now. My biggest girl, Caroline ... sort've helps now. Sorta. Mostly it's the old man: me, myself, and I out there." He laughs. An ugly, low laugh. Then, "Cindy does haircuts. Good ones. And she always loved to make these little things with the kids and her sister's kids ... decorations for Easter 'n' stuff." He snorts at the wonder of this. "She's a very celebratin'-type lady. And uh ..." He squints. "She dances good. She shakes everything." He flutters his eyes.

Connie is a little dumbfounded. But only for about five seconds. She recovers. "Well ... she must be upset right now."

He lowers his eyes. He watches Duane licking his swastika. He says a few shades more hoarsely, "She was upset *before*."

Connie sighs. "I'm sorry. What was wrong?"

"Our life. The shit. She's had to get the jobs."

His chatty pleasant expression leaves his face, a look

that makes Connie very nervous. A look she's never seen on a man's face. Only in movies. A bloodless, pissed-off tightening of the lips. Jaws clenching. Meanwhile, Connie is bursting with questions, and a girlish intimacy. Like with her two best friends. Aren't personal questions of strangers rude? How is it that this guy makes her feel both wretchedly nervous and sweetly intimate?

"A job?" she asks.

"Right."

"Well, that's wonderful. Don't you want her to have a job?"

"No."

"Why not?"

"It's fucking killing her." He looks directly in her eyes, his jaws still clenched.

Connie laughs lightheartedly. Makes a dismissive gesture. She knows the cold edge she's balancing on. She almost knows the answer. She just wants that most dark voice of Robert Drummond to speak, and to see the lined skin between his eyebrows bunch up tighter. "A woman," she presses on, "needs a career as much as a man does, Robert. What is Cindy doing? Does she like it?"

"McDonald's."

"Oh! Well!" she almost sings. "That can be fixed! What education does she have? Sometimes a couple of years—"

"You like questions," he says pleasantly.

"Well—" She laughs. "I just wanted us to talk."

He nods.

Duane moves up a notch, on toward the devil's left big toe.

Connie leans forward into what is really Robert's

space, close to the smell of his skin, the cigarettes—and a fresh bright green marijuana smoke smell—and she says with a funny little confessional smile, "I am a liberal."

Robert grins. "Why, shucks."

A hurried rumble outside that Connie knows is the UPS truck swinging up into the Creightons' brick driveway to the Stable, then the engine shutting off a little too suddenly as it always does. And Robert glances once in that direction, then back at Connie with a shy, apologetic smile and says, "I hardly ask people questions. I don't know. It's just the way I am." He pulls Duane down, ruffles the coarse gray-and-peach-streaked top of his head between the dark upright ears. "See ... I never woulda found out you was a liberal unless you just opened up with it yourself." His eyes widen playfully.

Connie leans back, eyes into his eyes. "I had to get it off my chest."

He looks at her chest. Very quickly. Looks away. Back to Duane, who is patiently starting all over again at the swastika.

Connie says softly, looking at her hands, which are picking at each other in her lap, "I sew, too."

"Neat."

"I've made lots of things. Shirts. Dresses. Kids' nighties and pj's. Infant layettes. I loved to do appliqué for a while. And years ago, halters ... when halters used to be the rage. I grew up in the sixties, a bit ahead of you."

"I remember halters," he says huskily.

Connie is seeing not her sewing machine and the slippery little halters she used to make that barely covered her nice big frisky breasts. What she is seeing is her husband's face. The way he is about sewing, about her garden, even about the children's books, which she has had some success with . . . what Jerry calls "storybooks." Jerry, that corporate lawyer, with a head for strategies. War in the courts. And now war in the Senate. The good wars. Civilized wars. The war of economics. The thing that distinguishes the better people is that your successes not be about bread and butter, but about power. No. Success is not about bread and butter, nor a pretty homemade skirt, nor a layette made for your best friend's twin babies. Not even those babies or your own baby, who grows into a dazzling, willful, beautiful daughter with a terrific Barbra Streisand–like singing voice, a fine modern dancer and pianist, with a love of teaching, and a tender heart. Annnd that daughter wins at chess. Beats everyone at chess! Even Jerry. Yeah, maybe Jerry was impressed by that. She remembers his earnest silence at that last Kristy versus Dad game where right to the finish, he tried. She could tell he was giving it his all, his mightiest all. And after the game, he stood up, peeled off his crew-neck sweater, and said, "Whew!"

Neither Connie nor Jerry would say they have marriage troubles. They get along. They laugh together. They understand that nobody is perfect. They are mature. And there is sex. Correct sex. Thoughtful sex. He always asks her if everything's OK. He always kisses her in a sweet way afterward. He always explains that he feels lucky.

So why is it she is spending less time in their gorgeous Washington apartment each year, practically settling here in Boston, a bit of clutter, the distinctive Massachusetts seasons ticking like the hours of a day through her blood. What part does a thing like "place" play in the mating game? Bread 'n' butter, competent hands, children, and

PLACE. Connie's eyes glide up Robert's darkly but sparsely haired muscular belly and chest, to his bearded chin, the few gray hairs that speak of his age ... which is ... yes, not a lot younger than her own age ... not a lot younger than Jerry.

With hesitancy Robert speaks, "Connie?"

"Yes?"

"Would you sew something for me?"

Her mouth actually drops open a little. There in his eyes a too-gleamy, mind-reading look, *perceptive*, more overstepping than any of her questions. She sees his left hand, which is powerful and effortless, draw Duane down from where Duane has started sniffing and lapping around the gauze and where the ghastly purpling of bruise marries and mixes with the garish tattoo flames. "Sure," says she. "What would you like?"

He reaches under his pillow and hands her the militia patch. "Kristy's gettin' me some clothes. If I could get that sewed onto one of my shirts. Left sleeve."

There is one spot of blood. On the E of the word MEN. SNOW MEN.

Connie smooths the patch out flat on her knee, her face stony. She had forgotten for as much as ten whole minutes about this part of Robert's story. Terrorist. Feelingless killer. Vengeful terrible man.

16

FIVE-THIRTY P.M. Dark. Noticeably darker earlier each week. Like a big gloved hand closing more completely over you if you were a bug. Another call from the FBI. A man with a very deep "grown-up" voice unlike the other caller. This man asks how long she and her daughter intend to remain in Boston? She explains they have no set time. He insists that until Robert Drummond is found, she will need protection.

She says, "Absolutely not."

He says that this is not a choice, that she has to accept this protection.

She is flabbergasted. The words *free country* come to mind. But that sounds so . . . so . . . right wing, doesn't it?

She holds her ground. And he backs off. Bye-bye. But as he is hanging up, he tells her he'll be getting back to her soon.

Around nine this evening, the gate buzzer in the kitchen goes off.

Connie knows it's them. She storms out into the yard,

down the brick driveway with a black Mexican shawl around her shoulders.

A car at the gates.

She hollers, "Thank you! But no!"

Driver's door opens and a medium-young man in a dark dress coat calls, "Mrs. Creighton, no one wants to disturb you. We're just letting you know we'll be near in case you need us."

Connie presses her lips together, sucks in her stomach. "Well, thank you. I appreciate it."

And she turns away and walks with great dignity back up to the door. Once inside that door, she lays her forehead against it and feels for the first time since Robert's arrival cold, clammy terror.

17

OVER THE NEXT few days, the FBI men are diligent. For a few minutes now and then, the street seems empty, but then it's not long before you see one of their cars down along the opposite curb, shadowy windshield showing no face. Once in a while, two cars will park out there. Sometimes three or four of these guys will stand out on the sidewalk in their dark dress coats or shirtsleeves and vests if it's warm, and talk and look around at roofs of neighboring houses, at hedges, at upstairs windows.

ONNIE AND KRISTY measure the third-floor windows for curtains, those windows not hidden enough by treetops, like the gable end of the study room and all of the living-room and kitchen dormers. At the fabric store Connie picks a light floral green fabric and a solid sunny yellow. She sews these curtains herself. Not sewing for babies. Not sewing for beautifying. This is *war*. So perhaps this sewing could be considered valuable?

19

UNMARKED GOVERNMENT CARS at both ends of the street. At Kristy's kitchenette table, a small wooden leaf table with delicate lathed legs, which Kristy and her mother had years ago painted a semienamel soft loden green and set under three tall skylights, which have three wide blocks of lemony light sifting down through the potted ivies and dresenas and dangling mobiles of copper and unpainted terra-cotta and Japanese glass to the chessboard below. A hand-carved chess set. Of a Roman style. The bishops and kings wear togas.

Robert doesn't sit but straddles his chair, which is backward, with his bad arm in its plaid sling draped across the back of the chair, chin on his forearm, his good arm reaching slowly and dramatically way out around the left flank of the board to suggest that this is guerrilla warfare.

Kristy's eyes are wide on the board. Her game. She has always been exceptional at chess. Not the world's champ or anything like that. But the champ of her boarding schools. And one of the three best players in her first years of college. This is Robert's second game. She let him win the first, helping him actually. Telling him the moves. Now on their second game, she's battling to win.

He is wearing his new jeans, socks, and sneakers. She found him a dark blue work shirt—Dickies—in a tiny clothing store in Cambridge. But he takes little interest in the shirts and T-shirts. She knows his shoulder hurts him fiercely. And his uncooperative right hand makes dressing a struggle. But she also surmises that Ruff Drummond likes to flash his tattoos.

She sees the ancient calendar sun face, green Christmas tree, and Grand Old Elephant descending slowly through her peripheral vision, big hand opening, and now Robert's muffled gentlemanly grunt, trying to hold back a real war cry, a yell of triumph as he pushes with two fingers his queen into the fateful foreground of her king.

Checkmate.

DOWNSTAIRS ON the sunporch, where her mother's easels and computers are—the two long plywood tables of paints and pastels and pencils, cozy chairs and papier-mâché elves, toads, and one big bright-eyed flying witch, here where Connie writes and illustrates her children's books—Kristy finds Connie reading a Russian novel with her rather Colonial-looking reading glasses. She wears her long robe of momentous magenta, legs outstretched on the ottoman. Legs in black tights. She looks content. If one can call this waiting-hiding game a thing of ease, a fruity margarita at an especially easy reach. Duane lolling on one of his doggie beds ... eyes open. Duane never really closes his eyes. Not tightly.

Kristy says deeply and icily, "He's won every damn game."

"How many is that, dear?"

"Seven. One after another. Bam! Bam! Bam! He's got so he puts me in check in the first eight moves." She unconsciously pushes at the ottoman with her toe, moving it a bit, then a bit more, Connie's outstretched legs and feet riding along.

Connie screws up her face. "That's amazing."

"He's scary."

"Yuh."

"I mean he's smart and scary."

"Our little Robert?" Connie chuckles deeply. "Is he showing signs of unpleasant self-importance?"

Kristy sighs. "It doesn't matter what he shows. He's thinking he's superior. Mr. Strategy. The male conqueror."

"Tsk. Tsk."

"There's no use playing with him. There's no game in it. So I put the board away."

Connie smiles down at her hands, fanning through the hundreds of flower-petal soft pages of the big novel. "Well, there's Scrabble. I'm sure you can beat him at that. He doesn't strike me as getting any high honors in the English language."

"Where is the Scrabble set?"

"In the children's guest room, in that hutch, I believe."

Kristy turns.

Connie says, "Sweetie, this isn't good for you . . . to be imprisoned here . . . by him. I want you to take my place at the Women's Literary Hour thing. It's Alice Walker. And Mary's coming for the film festival. Please go with her and Carl to that."

"Carl." Kristy makes a face like the face Robert made for AIDS.

"Remember! Sticks and stones!" Connie sings this.

When Kristy gets back upstairs, Robert is sitting in the center of the two-cushion love seat in her little living room, his legs apart, TV remote in his good hand, eyes on the screen. Oprah. With a close-up woman's face talking about her husband's hellish struggle with drugs and the ruination of their family because of "drugs." When Kristy appears in the doorway with the Scrabble set under one arm, clearing her throat meaningfully, a look of eminence upon her long pretty face, he raises the remote flicker, points it at the TV, his eyes still on the TV woman's big close face, and powerfully and, yes, violently, works the buttons, making the channels flash, pop, burp, burn, cluck, and hiss, then off. Drops his hand. Looks up at her gravely, says, "Your father. He's coming next week."

"But he never comes up to this floor. Never. Not even when we had this apartment done, when Mom and I were up here all the time painting and decorating. I always go downstairs to see him. As far as I know, he's never been up here, even when they were buying the house."

He looks back at the blank TV screen, the reflection of a curtained dormer on its surface. He looks back at her, not at her face or the pale mint green camp shirt or small gold sunburst medallion in its open collar, nor the Scrabble box under her arm, but at the whole picture of her, the way he had looked at the chessboard and saw every possibility, saw all her yet-to-be-made moves.

They set up the Scrabble board on the little green table. The sun has moved on. But the light is still inspiring. There is a sweet odor rising from a wooden bowl on the counter. Two pears. One fresh. One already having spent time here. Both of them an exotic dappled kind, ruby red. This bowl and a small stack of videotapes sliding away out of the pale shadow into darker shadow.

Kristy makes an herbal tea for herself. Gets Robert a

glass of bottled water. He is looking tired. He, in fact, looks flushy, fevered. But she says nothing about that. And neither does he.

A half hour into the game, it is evident he is winning. With carpentry words, car parts, farming implements, meat-cutting words, hunter terminology, parts of guns, Civil War—era terms, tools used by American Indians, and Indian architecture. "Those aren't words. Those are terms," she firmly insists, her voice a bit teacherish. She flaps through the weighty dictionary, heavy as a small child on her thighs. And there they are, his words.

A moment later. "Chainfall," says he. "C-H-A-I-N-F-A-L-L."

She is upset but plays it cool. "That's not a word, Robert."

"Well, i' 'tis. It certainly is."

"No. It is not!"

"Don't get upset, dear. It's just a game. It doesn't really matter." He calls her "dear" a lot. He calls everybody "dear." Kristy hates it, feels it is patronizing. But it's just Maine. Family, neighbors, all those endeared. Young and old. Male and female. In the South everyone is Ma'm or Mister. In Russia you are Comrade. In Australia it's Mate. In Maine, you are "Dea'eh."

"Yes, it does matter," she says a bit gravelishly.

"Why?"

"It just does." And she has tears in her eyes.

He pats her hand.

Phone rings.

She yanks her hand back. "Don't patronize me, Robert!"

Phone rings again.

He squints. "What's that mean?" He seems upset now, too. Flustered.

"It means treating me like an empty-headed idiot!"

Another half ring of the phone, then the answering machine does its job. Voice of one of Kristy's Pennsylvania friends murmurs from the study room. Kristy ignores the friend.

He decides to let her win. Then as she's so obviously doing better, she glares at him. "You are letting me win! THAT is patronizing! The worst patronizing!"

"I'm sorry," he says. "I didn't know it was patronizing. Baby, I'm just a dumb fuck. I don't know all your Ms. stuff."

She slams her chair back, stands, covers her face with her fingers, but screams through the fingers, "Get out! Get out! Get out of here!"

He gets up slowly, his face wooden, soldierly, just standing there with the fingers of his damaged hand moving slightly at the end of his sling, his good left arm hanging. He just looks at her, taking it. Under the brightness of the skylights, his eyes aren't just brown. But vivid, chestnut brown splotches around the pupils, drifting in green, with a narrow, razor-sharp, dark brown outer ring that gives each eye its odd aspect, creepy and beautiful.

After studying him a few moments through her fingers, Kristy drops her hands, looks down at the game board with all its intersecting words and solid little wooden letter tiles, always so satisfying to press between fingers. Softly, "It matters, Robert. Because it's significant. In life ... you know what I mean?" She looks at him. "Losers get trampled."

"Do you want me to leave this house now? I will. No problem."

"You can't."

"I can. I can just go down those stairs and out one a them doors. I gotta do it sometime. I can't stay forever inside this house. I can go today as well as next week or next month. I can."

"No." She looks at him tearily, a little smile of contrition. "Robert, I'm trapped here, too. I can't leave, either. I have so many decisions to make . . . about . . . my life. I'm here to make those decisions . . ."

She almost hears him ask, *What's wrong, dear?*, but he hasn't spoken. Only the creepily penetrating eyes have made this tender query.

Now back to tears, with shaking voice, "You don't know me, Robert. I'm not myself. I'm not like this ordinarily. I'm having a breakdown or something. I've been seeing a doctor for a few months. It's been difficult. But now . . . I can't believe this! I'm acting twelve years old! Please, Robert, see that this isn't me. It's like I'm all opened up. Like a shellfish that's scooped out . . . just all out there . . . quivering. And I can't keep up . . . with it all. So much to decide. The direction of things. And my doctorate . . . when I have that . . . where it'll take me. Where I should live eventually . . . options that are there . . . so many drawbacks. I say, Well, how about here in Cambridge-Boston area . . . Harvard, Amherst, Brown, Radcliffe . . . of course Radcliffe . . . Then, oh, the Midwest is . . . well . . . I'd rather settle in Northern California. I have friends out there. But Europe! My mother still has hordes of pals in France . . . wonderful people. You wouldn't believe how wonderful the French are." She stops, swallows. Done.

She is hugging herself tight. Such a tall long-waisted girl. The effect is shattered grace.

Robert squints, quietly confounded. Then, "Well." He breathes good and deep. "Here we are. Damned if we ain't."

OUT ALONG THE CURB, several unmarked government cars are parked. Are there people inside them? At this angle, you can't see any faces. Could be just a bunch of empty cars, except that there is that chilly feel of the eye, the eye of the thing that's bigger than you or I. And why are there twice as many cars? What has increased their fascination?

22

H E LIES ON HIS BED by the dormer with the clearly defined shadows of spruce trees shivering upon the floral print sheets and across his useless hand. His constant pain is like C-clamps tightening on the mangled muscle and nerve, glowing and shrill ... the scabbed-over skin itchy as hell. And his recurring little fevers make him at times both restless and exhausted. He is thinking of his brother-in-law, his sister's husband, Kevan. Dead. He sees Kevan dying. Dropping like a rag outside the Parker House. He hears the other shots next, knowing they are all dead, old friends he has gotten on with all his life, and then Frank, young, not a talker, just shy and careful. He feels again that punch to his shoulder and sees the mess come out through the front of his shirt and out of his sleeve. But he is still running hard. Run, Ruff, run. Sure dog. Heavy dog. Dizzy dog. Dying dog. You never expected roses today. Car horns. A staggering zigzagging trail of blood ... How is it that goes? ... You find water to get lost in, then sniff your way to the next stop, home of Jerry Creighton, "the Liberal." And so he got farther from them, closer to here. No talent. Just luck. And cold, cold rage. "Die, fucker, die," the last words from his throat and the good feel of the trigger, its familiar little play before it resists the finger...like a dog, yeah, a dog biting down on a bone. BANG!

He thinks of his people. His sisters and brothers, nieces and nephews, neighbors, old buddies, and Uncle Mike—his mother's uncle, great uncle to everybody else. Still keeps a farm. Somehow. And he thinks of Cindy and his daughter Caroline, sixteen this summer, takes after her old man, loves the outdoors, but...not home. School sports. Running, jumping, kicking, butting. And Josh, his boy. The oldest. The firstborn. He can't quite make out Josh's face for some reason. And the longing is hotter than anything in this room, anything under this gauze bandage or against this sheet, sun or flaming flesh. He thinks about death. Death in general. The place of death. The place where no one knows you. He thinks about cops. Their hands on him. Sooner or later, dead or alive. If he lives, they will beat the shit out of him in places that won't show. Don't cops just love to bash you when you're cuffed. He's heard it all. And now it will be his. A cell. Filth. Guards who make you squat and bend over. Claustrophobic airless leisure. Court. And more leisure.

And a weird public death.

Then he sees Cindy at McDonald's smiling at all of them in the line, day after repetitive, defining day, her face lowering as she taps out the items of the order. Smiling is not one of the hard rules of this job. None of the others smile. But Cindy, it's the right thing by Cindy. The thing you do. He sees the really stupid cap and outfit they make her wear. He sees her look up across at him as he waits by the nearest glass doors with four-year-old Ariel jumping around him on one foot, Ariel, begging for some new thing, something breathlessly advertised, or just leaning against him if she's tired, pouting, though sometimes she just nuzzles his sleeve. He cups this child's head, palm at the base of her skull, and looks into his own yearning eyes. He then looks up, sees his wife's face again, her numb despair, her wacky schedules, long, long drives to and fro, sometimes only one truck between them, or one car, whichever one runs. He sees her weary aging, her emptiness, her entrapment. Weep, Cindy, weep. Little foxy sweet lady in the trap. Oh, my love, little foxy foot in the steely grip, little foxy light-stepping foot broken there, hot in the trap, little bit a broken foot, little foxy weep woman weep. Blueberries on the mountain falling to earth. Blueberries in the sun. Quiet kitchen table, covered with homework, no meals. Little half-done bright dress jammed under the Singer's presser foot, never to be complete. And he sees it through his own exhaustion, too many jobs, too many begging voices, more bad news, more stuff coming down.

Cindy smiles at another customer. The smile lines around her mouth cut as if into oak or steel . . . the forty billionth hamburger, her one thousandth smile. The number of surpriseless hours uncountable. The five dollars that each hour represents already spent.

This isn't what we dreamed.

This isn't what we were promised.

He sees before he pulls the trigger, the back of the senator's graying head, with the Blackhawk's barrel driven against the skull, more like a spear than a gun, the man on his knees, the man who is whimpering, shivering, pissing down through his suit pants leg onto the marble floor, the flicker of light from the street through the brass supports of the revolving door, which someone has set into motion, changing the guy's gray hair to a whiter gray, almost dazzling, then back to streaky gray. And gripping the guy in place, the hands of Kevan, Frank, and John, everyone in that inarticulated pale feelingless daze of battle. And now he does it. He squeezes the trigger. Two times then. Two times now. So that on the sheet his hand actually moves. "Die, fucker, die."

23

SHE HAS SHUT the door to her bedroom, now changing into something different. Little brown sweater vest over a white linen blouse. She plans to go shopping. Let Connie and Art and Mark wait on "the guest." Connie is right. Getting out will be very, very good. And she'll stop in at the agency and see if Greta, whom she hasn't seen in six years, wants to see a movie, then maybe check out some Thai food. Something coconutty and veggie-ish.

She checks to be sure everything is in her bag. Suddenly a student pops into her head. Andrea. Young, of course. And yearning to please her. Remarkable essays and Andrea's round face, gold barrette on one side of her hair. Brown hair. Shy looking. But not shy. No, Andrea is confident. From a long line of A-plus professional people. But, yes, dying to please Professor Creighton, so at times there's a hint of groveling about her face and posture that could be mistaken at first for shyness.

Kristy sees the essays in stacks. Andrea's essay glows. And then Rachel's—her essays, her questions, her ideas . . . luminescence. But the rest of the students. Ordinary. Forgotten.

Some will go on to teach.

Education. Is education what education is really about? Knowledge? Wisdom? To become sagelike?

Meritocracy. The word spelled out on little ivory-color tiles.

And in the school cafeteria there was so much to choose from. One of the nation's best college cafeterias it was said. It had won some prize. But her favorite thing was just a sandwich. Herbal tea. A ripe banana. Many of the tables were made so that your chair faced the half-wall planter, one chair, one small table. For studying while you ate. She sees the hallways. The Quad. An almost make-believe green. Brochures and catalogs showed it even greener.

She sits on the bed to change her shoes but just stares stupidly at her left bare foot.

She feels both trapped and floating in space. Like Major Tom in that song from the seventies.

Trapped?

As professor of women's studies and department chair, she is *somebody*. She doesn't despise college life, does she? Awakening all those young minds to . . . to . . . thought? Everyone *thinks*. Pigeons think. Well, how about awakening young minds to knowledge? To achievement, to that higher plane. Is knowledge a synonym for achievement? There's a sour note here, too.

She remembers once talking all night with her ex-boyfriend Jared about the difference between a leader and a bully. People follow a leader. A leader inspires. A bully pushes, herds, terrorizes.

Her therapist here—whose name is also Kristy, but short for Krista instead of Kristina—tells Kristy that she, Kristina, fears success, a typical woman thing. But Kristy says, "Success is not the issue. Education is. And honesty. See what I mean?"

The therapist smiles indulgently but kindly...and personably. Kristy really likes this therapist. They are kind of like friends, but...

"Tell me about that then," instructs the therapist.

But Kristy's train of thought has zigzagged back to "success." OK, she fears success. If you could only plant "success" like a seed, water, weed, give it a little cowshit. But "success" isn't like that...unless you count shooting woodchucks that sneak into your garden. "Success" can only be stolen or won. Hoarded. Bitterly guarded. For every winner, how many losers?

Her therapist tells her that that is a typical "woman's concept" of success. Fearing rejection of the losers, or simply worrying about others too much, to the point of sacrificing your own abilities to make something of yourself.

Everything this therapist is saying Kristy has heard over and over and over. It is the feminist creed, is it not? The very feet and legs of all her own teachings, like cutting the chains of slaves, a merciful thing...all those female millions hiding behind their appliances or, worse, wallowing in poverty, needing only to be given beneficial slaps to the face, to send them onward and upward to the nice fat sky, the thrones of power stuffed with greedy men. Throw the men out! Grab those thrones! Claw! Scramble! Scrape. Stand erect. Someday you will rule!

The capitalist creed. Was feminism created in the image of the big "C"?

Winners. Losers.

Education. It keeps coming back to that ... "education." Where are the true sages? Where is the knowledge passed on for its own sake, lessons in parables, and how to wield a necessary life-sustaining tool, the knowledge of a tribe, a nation, a people, an equal people? Education shared. Passed 'round the circle.

She sees the institutions of education. Education created as a gray DNA of the institution, the System, the hierarchal lonely vertical machine.

She thinks about that word. M-E-R-I-T-O-C-R-A-C-Y laid out on the Scrabble board as it had been with Robert's C-H-A-I-N-F-A-L-L, intersected with it, wedded to it.

"What's a chainfall, Robert?" she'd asked.

"It's what you hoist a deer or calf up with when you skin 'em."

24

THEY CATCH HER EYE as she is walking briskly past shop-windows. Military clothes and boots. Camo and olive drab, khaki and even SWAT black. Camping equipment. Mysterious gadgets. She sneaks a peek down the narrow street, then across the street and behind her. Nobody seems to be watching her. Or pretending not to be watching her. She goes into this small but packed store, lit in ultimate fluorescent, fluorescent designed to make even a skin pore look like a deep well. Peaches-and-cream faces transformed into blistering pimple purple. But she loves the smell of this store. She sees everything but blood and guns. Everything that *goes* with blood and guns. Compass watches, first-aid kits, sunglasses, walkie-talkies, knives, vests with a dozen pockets, bandoliers, wilderness and military binoculars, aviator-style hearing protectors for the ears—to protect your ears from the sound of gunfire—cardboard boxes of MREs, coffee-colored wool blankets, camo mattresses, camo sleeping bags . . . now racks of military boots and over these racks, flags spread on the walls, American flag, Confederate flag, POW-MIA flag (*You Are*

Not Forgotten). And Special Forces flag, which is a skull wearing a beret. (*Kill 'em all. Let God sort 'em out.*)

Shirts and pants. Camo for desert. Another camo for jungle. Another for forest. She picks up a forest camo shirt, sniffs its satisfying newness. Size: SMALL. She flips folded shirts around, hunting for his size. Easy to find. An ordinary man. Medium in every way.

When Kristy takes the shirt to the counter, she sees that the clerk has a video screen of all the aisles, so that she was able to watch Kristy as Kristy browsed. The clerk has red squiggly hair, a short person, thickset and young. She does not wear anything that looks like it came from this store. Her blouse is peppered with little planet Earths and Saturns and Plutos. She doesn't smile. As she takes the shirt and credit card, stuffs the shirt into the bag, she doesn't even look at Kristy. It's as if when she got a look at Kristy through the video screen, that was good enough.

ONNIE AND DUANE are out in the garden, Connie filling several cardboard boxes with dry statice and baby's breath, and other nice things for making flower arrangements for the Boston Women's Club affair, and a few for the house and for Jenny, her old friend, back from Hollywood again, smashed by Hollywood, Hollywood nothing like what it used to be, even though Jenny was getting even better than she used to be. She and Jenny will read a play together around the fireplace at Jenny's, and hopefully, Phyllis, each reading two or three parts... depending. Connie, with her deep voice, always offers to do the men's parts. Phyllis is Jenny's lover. Twenty-five years Jenny's senior and a Communist, a real Communist, not a lip-service Communist, not an aspiring Communist... She was a secretary of the Party, red-baited, blacklisted, jailed, and yet still good-humored.

She hears Kristy's Porsche out on the street, slowing, the gates opening with a little lively shiver.

The day is turning. The humid heat is back. Hurricane

weather. Hurricanes come with such cute names, like friendly giants . . . very friendly, very clumsy giants.

Kristy tells her she saw no cars parked on the street when she came in. No FBI, nothing.

Connie replies by just making a weary face.

Kristy shows her the camo shirt.

Duane sniffs the air.

"Well, well, my, my," chortles Connie approvingly. "That's kind of coincidental. It's just what I needed."

Kristy giggles incredulously. "Not for you, Mom! It's for—"

"I know. I know." She lowers her voice, whispers, "What I mean is I have a sewing project he asked me to do that requires just such an article as this." She holds the shirt up to herself, while explaining about the patch he'd given her.

The blue, gold, ivory, and pale pink splotches of color around Connie's garden wink in the changing light.

Duane has many great holes around which he has been working on through the summer but finds he needs to start another one over by the plum tree.

Kristy confesses what happened with the Scrabble game. The whole scene.

Connie sighs, gives the shirt a frisky, scolding shake.

In a suddenly high, creaky, childly voice, Kristy says, "Mom?" and steps close and Connie, stuffing the shirt under one arm, hugs her daughter hard, rocking her from side to side, Connie's big breasts soft as pillows, and Kristy taller than her mother, but being a little crimply-kneed now, therefore of less stature. And Connie takes Kristy's face in her hands and kisses the white, wonderful forehead, the sweet, dark widow's peak. And she speaks in a raspy outlaw whisper, "I'm glad you came home." "Home" meaning Boston. Yeah, not Washington. A subtle confession? And home meaning home from Pennsylvania, which is a really outrageous thing to say or to feel or to wish for. You are not supposed to want your grown child home or near home. It's not healthy. Career comes first. There are so many things to confess, so many things wrong these days that were once right, were once the mother's gift, the child's gift, the family's glory.

And Connie says it again, "I'm glad you came home. Even to this."

ON ONE OF THE networks, commentators and "expert" guests discuss the motives of Robert Drummond and his militia. They are trying to figure out these crazy people, especially Drummond: What his parents probably did to him or didn't do or the grudges he held against schoolteachers and therefore authority or what lax gun laws have allowed. The effects of "a violent society," a "military-worshiping society." Violence in the schools. Permissiveness in the schools. Insufficient funding of schools. Drugs. Drugs, of course *drugs*. And what can be done to stop the wacko right wing . . . to stop the Militia Movement.

A large pink-faced man and a slim dark-skinned woman, both professionals in the mental health field, are joined by one nondescript sociologist, a bright-eyed DA's assistant, a social worker wearing black, and a man named Mo Pease, head of the Southern States against Right-Wing Aggression Center, to discuss again without actually speaking the F-word, the fact that Drummond had screamed, "Clear out!! Clear those people out!! This fucker's gonna ricochet!!" and then "Die, fucker, die." The first "fucker" referred to the about-to-be-discharged gun, the bullet actually. The second "fucker" referred to the senator. The experts on the panel all agree on this.

It is also noted that most right-wing Christians wouldn't say that word—that word no TV people are allowed to say, either.

A lot of nods.

Cautiously and deliciously the panelists work through the hypothetical corridors of the killer's psyche. When the time comes, if Drummond is brought alive into custody, whole teams of psychiatrists and psychologists will be deployed to explore this man's dark mind.

If he comes to them dead, nevertheless, whole teams of psychiatrists and psychologists and liberal experts on right-wing thinking will be deployed through a galaxy of media to explore other people's memories about who Robert Drummond was and why he did it. And then to play the composite expert voice again and again and again for as long as profitable. Understand this, the institutional, the expert, the assessed, the educated guess is the only reality and therefore singular, and then into the future this will be condensed into a one-liner of conventional wisdom for all and therefore will be the actual Robert Drummond.

27

ND THE UNMARKED government cars parked outside the Creighton home wait. In front of the house and on the other street behind the backyard as well.

Day.

Night.

Day.

Night.

A constant protective ring like the eyes and ears of a parent. Like the loyalty of an old friend. Like the hard squeeze and hot breath of a pet gorilla.

28

I N A MOMENT alone in the shadowy, heavily draped library, Connie asks Kristy if maybe she'd like to sleep downstairs in one of the ell guest rooms. "Sometimes it's a little nerve-racking having your only daughter sleeping upstairs in the same attic as a fugitive killer."

Kristy says flatly that she's not afraid.

Connie insists, "Even good decent men might... have... funny ideas in the night."

Kristy says, "Robert... is... good. And decent. OK?"

Connie's top lip trembles a bit, a facial thing she's had since childhood when she is flustered.

Kristy says, "So what are you worried about... him killing me?... or fucking me?"

Connie says calmly, "Force. I'm concerned about force."

Kristy cocks her head. Flutters her eyes. "Maybe I want him to... fuck me."

"OK!" says Connie brightly, throwing up her hands. "As long as everybody is happy!"

WITH THE HOUSEKEEPER gone now on her surprise vacation, Connie takes all the downstairs calls herself, and the high-tech pulsings of these phones are getting on her nerves as she tries to work a little on her koala book. This morning a neighbor, Margaret Dealer, calls to ask if the FBI agents have visited with her yet. Connie says lightheartedly, "They better not! I am an artist! They interrupt my artistic flow, and I'll sue the pants off them!"

The neighbor laughs a little. Then says, "We are all a little fidgety, Connie. Why do you suppose the FBI is talking with all of us over here? They have been to quite a few homes here, we're coming to discover. When the two gentlemen were here, I couldn't pin them down on this...but it's apparent to us that they suspect that that psychopath is going to try to get some of us next. With his twisted mind, he probably has it out for all people of means."

Connie snorts. "The FBI just wants to look busy. Probably Robert Drummond has actually escaped to the Bahamas. I'm not worried."

After the call, she gets herself a *real* drink. A Black Russian. And she sits alone in the larger parlor drinking it without tasting it.

ANOTHER DAY. He sits in a chair, a big antique Boston rocker in the larger parlor with Duane on his lap, Duane staring into his eyes, Duane whose allegiance to Robert has grown beyond duty, into the realm of liturgy.

Robert wears his new dark blue work shirt tucked into his belt, the new jeans and sneakers, his hair combed with water, parted carefully on one side, looking ready for a day's work that he will never make it to. His bad arm is motionless in its plaid sling. He strokes Duane's coarse fur with his good left hand and now watches Connie across from him on an elegant mauve upholstered antique thing, hand-sewing his militia's patch onto the left sleeve of the new camouflage-spotted shirt. Her fingers are deft at this. He likes the look of her fingers doing this. And the way she breaks thread with her teeth. It makes her seem powerful, motherish . . . a little bearlike.

With her deepest voice, she says, "You've been smoking grass with my daughter, haven't you, Robert?"

This voice has caused her to seem less motherish; instead, schoolteacherish and self-righteous and threatening. He wants to answer with "So what?" but swallows, then says with a sheepish smile, "She has the best I've ever had."

Connie snorts at this. She would like to get him to talk. She loves to hear his aristocratic "ahf-tah" for *after* and mumbled "rud" for *road*. Before Robert she never heard an accent like that. Only people whose "education" had diluted theirs. Or the horrible cardboard versions by Down East humorists.

Sometimes Connie stares a little too hard at Robert's mouth.

Duane shifts from foot to foot on Robert's lap, his feet very small, but his chest and shoulders broad and terrierish. Robert feels the shape of the small foxlike head, feels the energy under his palm like an underground spring or river or sea. Or the way the million million million stars cannot be detected with the naked eye by day.

Connie asks Robert what he likes for music. For a minute they talk about music.

She asks who his heroes are. He replies, "Subcomandante Marcos and Nestor Cerpa."

"And who are they?"

"Militia," Robert answers with his teeth and tongue doing something that makes this single word seem thicker. The two names just don't have a Maine ring to them. Nor a Montana ring to them for that matter. Maybe Texas. "Friends?" she asks.

His eyes glitter on her a long moment. "Maybe."

She asks about his kids, if they get good grades in

school. He scoffs at the idea of good grades, makes that same face he'd made when Kristy had told of the vet's concern about AIDS.

She asks if his wife is a good cook.

He says, "I don't know. I guess. She don't burn nuthin'."

"What about you?"

"Cook?" A flicker of the same AIDS/school-grades face. Then he gives a little dismissive spit of a laugh. Some might take this as his scorn for "women's work." Others might take it as self-scorn. Whatever you seek, you shall find it.

She describes the herbs in her garden, explains how she uses them in her cooking.

She promises to make him something nice tonight, that she sees no reason why he can't come downstairs and eat in their dining room. If anyone comes to the gates but Art or Mark, there will be a buzzer. She and Kristy can have a nice dinner party for him with all sorts of goodies.

"Gourmet," she tells him. She sees that his eyes are on her hands, admiring. His eyes in this shadowy, heavy room—tall windows curtained and draped to the max— seem quite a nice dark brown. She asks, "How do you feel now? I know you've been getting those little spells in the afternoons . . . usually . . . don't you?"

He shrugs, making a tough it-ain't-nuthin' gesture with his hand.

She tells him a little about Jerry, about when they were first married, how he used to be quite the sport fisherman. "Maine . . . he loved Maine. And Alaska. He would fish till he dropped. And sailing. He's still quite the sailor." She says Jerry is color-blind, which is hard for her, being an artist and wanting his full appreciation of her work.

Robert looks down at Duane, and Duane flattens his foxy ears, perks them up, flattens them, perks them, attuned to Robert's every gesture.

Connie rethreads her needle, again biting the thread.

Robert says evenly, "FBI fuckers have devices now where they can hear every word we're saying. You can bet they know I'm here."

Connie makes a face. "Robert, I doubt they've gotten that sophisticated."

"Well, they certainly have. They can hear over quite a distance. Where've you been? They even showed it on the educational channel. The distance from that street to anywhere inside this house is nothing for them. They know I'm here. They're just playin' their friggin' games with us."

Connie is silent now. Her terror and confusion swim like dark stripy fish all around this silent room.

Robert stares at Connie.

By the time she's ready to rethread her needle, she has convinced herself that such hearing devices are just part of Robert's paranoia... the "ultra-right-wing paranoia"... goes with black helicopters... goes with advancing Russian armies on the Mexican and Canadian borders. She says brightly, "I used to teach school! Fourth graders."

Robert's eyes widen, then narrow. "Guess you done a lotta things in your life," he says coldly.

"Mmmmmmmmmm-hmm." Then she asks about his parents.

Both dead. Father died in his fifties. Aneurysm. Ugly but fast. His mum died slow. Recently. Died in a nursing home. "We couldn't take care of her anymore. Too busy chasin' the dollar." He tells how he and Cindy and the kids lived in the farm place where he grew up. Thirty acres. His home. All his brothers and sisters had gone to live in their own houses nearby, all married. One went upstate. But he and Cindy stayed on, to take care of the place, keep it up, and to be with his "mum." But when his mother had her second stroke, Cindy was already forced to take two jobs—two part-time jobs—and nobody was around to help his mother. "And she got really mental. We think it got to be more than strokes. I don't know what. But she weren't that old. And the state took the farm from us to pay for the nursing home. Took our home. Fuckers."

"It's hard. But probably it would have made your wife feel held down to be home all day with a sick old woman," Connie presses, knowing, knowing him now, knowing the dark anger she can make happen on his face.

He sits up straighter. "Held down?"

"Yes. A man doesn't realize how a woman needs to spread her wings like he does. But it's true." She doesn't look up at him as she reaches to put the thread down.

Deadly silence from Robert's corner of the room, not even the creak of his rocker or the rustle of his fingers through Duane's strawlike fur. She looks now. Robert's face is terrible. Like a man who pulls the trigger on a man who is being held down on his knees. She asks, "What's wrong, Robert?"

"Let me get this straight with you," he says. "Cindy loves old people. So maybe she could drive an extra hour and a half each way to go work in a nursing home, maybe the same one, maybe not, that's not up to us, anyway...Mum goes off to whichever one she gets let into 'cause no one's home at our house and the nursing home makes a hundred bucks an hour and the state pays them and then takes our farm, which I put every penny of mine into for years keepin' it up...and so now we got nuthin' but a little shit shack and three kids all in one bedroom and us on the couch and a brand-new mortgage, which is breakin' us, and we've started to say...uh, yuh, time to go look for a fuckin' fire hydrant to live in the shade of!"

He stands up, setting Duane down on the warmed rocker pillow, and turns to face Connie, who is not sewing anymore, just looking at her hands with the shirt-sleeve and militia patch rumpled between them, and Robert's eyes are black, fiery, and bottomless.

"Held down, you say? Cindy and I've both been held down, Ms. Creighton. Ain't no wings spread, hers or mine. Just held down. Held down to her little piss-poor jobs and mother-fuckin' big corporation big-profit power fuckers instead a makin' her own life, held down by management shitheads orderin' her and the others around like cattle...the clock...the fuckin' clock like a big fuckin' rock tied to her neck...and me an' my shit's goin' down...Nobody's buildin' 'cause everyone's goin' down strugglin' to get along, Connie...so we are all slavin' just to make the big guys rrrrricher. So I get FOUR little diddly-squat piss-poor temp machine-shop jobs... nooooo benefits....that means nooooo insurance, no doctors, no female exams for Cindy, no way I can get this hernia I got patched up, no way 'cause we spent hundreds already on Caroline's eye operation and glasses and Josh's wrist...gettin' worried now 'bout teeth, which was all pretty good teeth before...but, well, let's see...gotta choose. Let's see ... teeth or female exam? Hernia or the leakin' roof? Manifold valve and exhaust system in the truck ... orrrrrr property taxes? Which? Which? Which? Pick one. Tomorrow it's somethin' else. Every day a new surprise!"

He pushes his good hand through his hair. He swallows hard, like swallowing a big gulp of water or warm tea. "So, I ..." His eyes sparkle. Tears. "An' so I work in the woods on the weekends with Kevan ... shovel roofs and pay bills pay bills pay bills, cost of everything goin' higher than a rocket while the fuckin' guv'nuh and legislature keep humpin' the big companies and sayin' to me and my people that if they bring morrrrre big companies to Maine, we'll all be in pig heaven or somethin' but all 'tis more of us draggin' our asses and our chains for 'em ... fast, faster, FASTER ... and lose more every day, lose our houses, lose our folks, lose our fuckin' freedoms, lose our fuckin' balls to 'em ... and the only thing that gets cheaper is what they pay us while the goddamn big-company socialists in the State House and where your boy is, those goddamn fuckers and the big-boy fucker in the White House and his arrogant bitch broad femmie-Ms. wifey and the banker boys eat my Constitution for breakfast and tell me I can't have a gun because I might fuckin' use it, baby, use it ... and all the while they're pullin' all our strings and sucking the last sweet dollar out of our hides! Held down?"

He steps closer to where she sits. "It ain't no man-woman thing a'tall. None of us like bein' fucked over. We're all on our backs! None of us like bein' fucked up the ass! An', Connie, don't gimme that shit about education fixin' this. We don't wanna be yuppies. We can't stand the sight of yuppies. The only education we want is to find out what the hell's really goin' on! We're sicka fairy tales! We want to be just ... be just us! And we wanna make it! An' to live where we are ... at home. And to ... see it ... you know ... the American dream ... which says, *Work your ass off, people, and you get what you deserve!* Fuckin' A! We shouldn't have to turn inta disgustin' icy yuppie pig shit to stay alive!"

Connie stands up, shirt done, Snow Men patch in place, her fingers trembling slightly, and she looks up at him and says softly, "I just wish ... the right thing could be done ... by peaceful methods."

He turns and squints at the closed drapes, beyond which is the quiet street, a single unmarked government car at the curb, and the ivy-grown arbor of the neighbor overway, while only a few streets up, the malady of horns and red lights and grinding gears and swarming anonymity of the heart of Boston. He speaks now in his softer, hoarser, gentler voice, "I've done the peaceful thing for forty-four years." He looks back at her face. "I sat for twelve fuckin' years in your schools and was a good little darlin' 'cause I didn't cause no trouble ... didn't break nuthin' ... didn't goof around ... just peace an' sweetness. But that wasn't enough! Not enough. They want you to study, study, study, do your tricks. Sit up. Beg. Roll over. Fill in the circles. Name in the left corner, not the right. No leaky penzzzzz. Then finally I get the hell out of there. I work. Watch a little TV. Raise my own meat and garden. An' pay my bills. Dress my kids nice. Load 'em on the meat wagon for school. School says get 'em computers. I get 'em computers. School says get 'em flutes and saxophones. I get 'em flutes and saxophones. I just goooo with the flow. Mr. Peace, that's me. And I've not seen one iota of change for the better in all those years of votin' and behavin' an' peaceful palaverin'."

Connie shakes her head gently. "There's a difference between peaceful activism and passive giving in. Remember every ripple . . ."

"Yeah, yeah, yeah. You got the answers. You see it all. You see it all." He pokes the slippered toe of her right sneaker with his left sneaker, not hard, but firmly. He looks into her green eyes, nice green eyes, eyes that hear him, are trying to feel it, trying . . . and he says, "Baby. You. Do. Not. See. It. All."

She presses the shirt against his good hand. He takes a hard, quick breath, like she just slammed the shirt into his stomach. His hand closes around the shirt, his one and only hand. Then he brings this hand, with the shirt dangling from it, around back of her shoulders and leans down and speaks gruffly against her cheek. "After my wife and I get over fights, I always put the meat to her."

Connie is confounded. Not at his words of sexual aggression, but at her response to it, which is nothing but a submissive wordless flush.

He smells like marijuana, but also of recent cigarettes, which she suspects Art gets him.

Now he steps away, so she can leave the room, which she does, briskly and ladylike. But Duane doesn't follow her. Duane stays with Robert, staring up at him, eyes filled with a world of respect.

ROBERT WEARS HIS camo shirt with militia patch tucked formally into the belt of his jeans, his hair combed painstakingly with water, sits at the head of the lace-covered long, long antique pine table, where usually sits the senator, "the Liberal."

The drapes are drawn tightly over all the windows.

On the mantel of the many-flued fireplace are dozens of small pictures and portraits, all handsomely framed. One shows the senator leaning against a shop doorway in some Europey place, a cart of bright fruits stage right front. He is wearing a funny hat. There is a series of photos in one frame of a preteen Kristy with a butterfly on her nose and a butterfly in the air, Kristy leaping, her face too earnest. No pictures show her delight. A photo in black-and-white of one of the senator's heroes, John Thomas Scopes, taken in the courtroom just after the verdict. And there's the family, young Jerry and Connie, with baby Kristina on a lap, all three figures dressed in white against an infinite black background, like substance versus emptiness, or flesh and fabric versus universe...or purity versus evil. An impressive artsy photo.

Robert has carefully studied all these photos, but he has also studied the whole room just as carefully: low ceilings, the way they made them in the 1700s, the simpler woodwork, door frames, door latches, windows, floors. He caresses wood and plaster. He squats down to finger the old broad-head floor nails and the way two odd-shaped wide boards are fitted together so ingeniously. Now seated at the table, Robert asks if Duane can sit in a chair next to him and have a little plate.

Connie and Kristy both look aghast. Connie and Kristy both despair that this could get Duane into a bad habit, but Connie goes to get a small utilityish sort of plate for Duane to use—"Not our china."

So now Duane stares up at Robert from his own nice armed chair.

Connie sees the square bulge in one of Robert's chest pockets. Cigarettes. Art actually confessed a few hours ago. So where Robert gets the cigarettes is no secret, but where he smokes them is the secret since Kristy claims she's never smelled smoke in any of the apartment rooms.

However, Kristy is lying.

With his good hand, Robert thoughtfully pulls at his dark mustache, fingers the graying center of his beard, and, studying Duane a long moment, declares, "He's just like in the *Wizard of Oz*, isn't he?"

"Yes," Kristy says with a nice laugh. "Like Toto."

"Run, Toto, run!" Robert calls in a squeaky voice.

Duane's ears flatten, then perk up, then flatten and perk up, one for each syllable spoken in Robert's new voice.

Both women have graciously remembered that Robert will probably want to say grace, being a right-wing radical person, and this is suggested with a bit of tongue-in-cheek as there is much doubt concerning Robert's strict adherence to Christian law.

And Robert says, "I don't really know any graces by heart."

Connie says deeply, "You are a Christian, correct? A strong Christian."

He flushes. "Yes."

Kristy narrows her eyes, fidgets with the sleeve of her harvesty orange-brown sweater top. "I don't believe you."

He looks sheepish. "I was married in a church...but mostly we never do church. No time. Just not enough time. Different weddings. Different churches. Funerals...that's church."

Kristy looks at her mother. "There is time for a lot of church for devoted Christians. They *make* time."

Robert agrees. He knows lots of people like that.

Connie taps the table, looking from face to face. "Then, Robert...you aren't full right wing."

He smiles, unfazed. "Guess not."

Connie and Kristy look at each other pleasantly.

Robert sits straighter. "Don't get excited, ladies. I ain't no atheist. I'm not one a you people."

Kristy folds her hands, squeezes her eyes shut. "Comrades, we will omit reading from the *Communist Manifesto* this evening and ask simply that whoever or whatever is listening to this prayer, hear that we are grateful for this food and your everlasting patience. Amen."

She opens her eyes, sees that Robert's are wide on her, a dark glare, but his head still dutifully bowed. She gives a little sniff of triumph and reaches for the salad bowl, which she passes to her mother with practiced grace, and stares into Connie's eyes, which are twinkling and appreciative of the moment.

And Robert says gruffly, "The FBI is listening, that's who's listening."

Connie says sadly, "Let's try to forget the FBI for a few minutes. Let's just enjoy."

Food is all over the place. Food steaming in herbed heaps on platters and under covers: Huge shrimps. Pasta and pesto. Sun-dried tomatoes. Light bread and heavy bread. Three salads. Grapes and Brie cheese rolled in nuts. Sweet potatoes glazed. Smoked salmon and funny meats. A great tray-sized spinach pie. Enough for a trainload of militiamen. But Robert's appetite isn't much tonight. He tries a spoonful of everything. He says, "No thank you, dear," warmly to the chardonnay that Connie reveals is "the best on the planet." But Robert insists it might clash "with all my vet'rinary pills."

They see that he is, yes, getting glassy-eyed and fever-flushed, more so by the minute. When Dr. Wood visited yesterday, he explained that Robert was still a very sick man and in more pain and discomfort than he lets on.

But he dutifully tries the dessert and asks if they'd keep "some of this stuff" for later. When he stands up to go to his bed, he asks if Duane can go up with him, keep him company.

This is agreed to.

A S A RULE, Connie is a late sleeper. She sleeps well, even though everyone warns her that impending menopause is going to keep her tossing. This morning while she is standing by the big messy bed—a king-sized bed (the senator has long legs and he always sleeps fitfully)—she sees a sheet of paper just inside the door on the wide pine-board floor. She finishes sashing her robe, then bends for the paper, her long sandy hair, unwound for the night, swings down as she reaches. She takes the paper to the light of a window and sees it is a drawing in a style much like the primitives. Some Russian artists come to mind. Here is a kind of artist for which no amount of training could ever undo that powerful raw childly edge. It is clearly a picture of herself, some sewing in one hand, a steaming pan in the other. Her face is rosy. Her eyes big and green. The ripply loose curls around her ears are dancing. Her feet, a little too big. Beside her stands a wolf. A wolf-sized wolf, but she knows it's Duane. The room around the two figures looks convex. The floor bulging up. The walls breathing. A fireplace of fire-engine red with a shadowy urgent mouth in the middle.

Under this picture in a careful but manly handwriting:

Thank You
Ruff

She stares a long moment at the picture and the words. Maybe the wolf is Robert.

33

IN A BARROOM in Boston a group of men and women, mostly men, are staring at yet another replay of the sidewalk outside the Parker House minutes after the execution-style assassination of Senator Kip Davies. Several sprawled bodies are strewn about on both the sidewalk and the street, a close-up of one with what looks like blueberry jam running from his mouth, nose, and empty left-eye socket. There's a militia patch on his left sleeve. A few flashes of the funeral of Senator Kip Davies, attended by dignitaries from all over the world, all the tight faces of the mourners, the half-mast flag, the drums, the guns banging off blanks, then a new photo of Robert Drummond, this one with a lever-action rifle, dead deer, deer hanging by a spreader through its rear tendons from a six-by-six timber between trees. Then closer, the face of Robert Drummond. Grave. Hard. Calculating. Menacing. Crazed. This is the picture the networks really love. As well as the composite witness sketch, which offers a machinelike countenance.

And now sketches of Robert Drummond's tattoos. The

camera hovers like a hornet on the swastika. Authorities now believe the killer is still in the Boston area. He is armed and dangerous, and anyone who has seen a man of this description is urged to contact authorities at once.

One of the men at the bar leans on his forearms and says, "I'd like to meet that guy. That took guts."

Another man says, "He looks like my boss. I been teasin' Jim since this happened. I say, 'Law's after you, Jim.' We all been gettin' a good laugh over that."

Bartender still staring at the TV, though it is now advertising insurance, says, "Militia Movement guys are pissed. They want to see Drummond fry. They're writing letters to all the papers asking that Drummond get fried fast . . . skip the appeals."

Everyone looks at the bartender with grave wonder.

Bartender goes on, "Militia Movement is about defense and defense only. And common-law court. They don't even like it when people organize demonstrations. Demonstrations are democracy. They say democracy is bad; democracy is chaos. They believe you stockpile, you study common law, you pray, and you wait. That's it." He turns from the TV, leans onto the bar. Pulls on his nose three or four times.

"What about Oklahoma City? That wasn't defense," offers a guy to the far right of the bartender.

Bartender sighs. "McVeigh was not militia."

"He was working with the government," another guy murmurs, too softly to be heard by all. "You look at replays of a film of that and you're gonna see there's no way McVeigh did that with a cowshit bomb. That was military. All four support columns popped all at once."

A guy who hasn't heard this soft-spoken guy offers,

"Militias get a bad rap. Now and then you get a renegade one or some right-wing individual gone berserk and the networks jump on it like a duck on a june bug."

A woman who is standing between two occupied stools places a bill on the bar, and while the bartender mixes up her usual drink, she says, "Robert Drummond. They should have a statue of him."

A croaky-voiced guy with as many tattoos as Robert Drummond has, only all in black, says, "Well, the militias can say what they want . . . but I myself wish Drummond's group had gone all the way to Washington with M-14-full autos and done the job right. If he's going to the chair, might as well get all he can get."

"Like I say, they oughta do a statue of him."

"They are not going to do a statue of him, Mag," groans the croaky-voiced tattooed guy, shaking his head, looking pained.

"I know. I'm just jokin'."

Bartender slides a blackish-brownish murky-looking drink toward the woman and says, "Militia Movement guys say Drummond's militia wasn't part of the Movement. They are making it real public that they disavow him. Mostly Internet. But they have been getting in some papers, too, which must mean bags and bags of letters are coming in from these guys. I saw one interview where the commander of a militia in Colorado is demanding that Drummond be publicly flogged before they put him to death."

Croaky-voiced tattoed guy says, "Now if I were Drummond, I'd lay low and maybe get plastic surgery and a hair dye!"

The woman keeps standing, snug between the two

occupied seats, sips her drink, then, "Did any of you guys see the *Circus of Horrors* back in the fifties?"

"No."

"No."

"Well, it had that 'Look for a Star' song as its theme, and every time I heard that song played, I got the creeps. I was really too young to've seen that thing. All it was was about this plastic surgeon who did deformed people and crooks. But the way they did it ... with music and whippin' off their veils, it was scary as hell."

Bartender snorts. Feels his clean-shaven jaws. "I don't think I'd want a new face even if it was the face of a god. It would be too weird."

"Well," says a man to the bartender's far left. "Maybe that is Drummond's thinking."

An oldish woman with glasses and an Elvis hairdo sitting next to this man who has just spoken looks hard at him and says, "Maybe he had the operation and he's you."

Everyone hoots and cackles over this.

Croaky-voiced guy says, "Robert Drummond is going to turn up floatin' in the harbor anyways. Whatya wanna bet?"

Bartender: "Unh-unh. Not so. Know why?"

"Why?"

"Because the government and the networks want to give us another big trial."

"I'm sicka trials," snarls the oldish woman.

34

OBERT AND KRISTY sit together in her living room
smoking a joint, Duane on Robert's lap. Robert
sprawls on one pillow of the love seat, one knee bent
sideways, one leg out straight. Kristy has pulled up a
rocker to face him, quite close. In fact, Robert's left foot
somewhat trigs her rockers. Duane likes this coziness. And
Duane sees nothing wrong with marijuana. Right now,
Duane sees nothing wrong with life.

Kristy tries to explain some of her problems to Robert.
Problems with few concrete details, mostly one fairly gaseous concept fuzzing into another gaseous concept, and a
lot of sighs.

Robert nods, inhales, holds his smoke, reaches across
to her with the joint, which she then holds in her lips as
he exhales, and he asks, "What's women's studies?"

Kristy holds her smoke, looking at her knee. She feels
lazy. She doesn't want to fight it now, to fight the rote, to
test the raison d'être of her peers, so easily spelled out, so
easy, so easy. She rides the rote like a good-feeling little

rocking horse. She floats the untroubled blue sea, hoping that Robert will, too. Her teacherly voice explains that it is the study of women placed in a positive light . . . *for a change.* "Women in power. Women who are successful. It is the reversing of various attitudes, misconceptions, and cultural wrong notions about women. I bring in a lot of guests who will be good role models. It can get quite academic. Comparisons—"

"You mean if there is a man in there . . . in the historical stuff . . . you erase 'im?"

Kristy, having passed the joint to him, now gets it back. "Yeah, sort of. But that's oversimplifying . . . maybe I'm sort of oversimplifying, too." She inhales deeply, then laughs out her smoke too soon. Then laughs again. "But we need to undo what men have done to us for centuries, since before Christ. In fact, Christ was modeled after the spirit of wisdom who was a woman. Many thousands of years ago, women were worshiped. Goddesses. Men hated that. Over time they—the men—did away with that so they could create a society in which women would be subservient, so that women would worship men . . . but men have failed. Everything has become . . . well, a violent, greedy, male-dominated society."

Robert is squinting.

Kristy, irritated by his exaggerated squint, just keeps on, ". . . therefore, we need to show women other women, just women . . . strong women . . . to compensate."

Robert has the joint now, and he's laughing and snorting and glancing at Duane in a conspiring-between-men sort of way. "Gettin' even with men," says he.

"No, Robert. Not getting even. *Compensating.*"

"So, do you have men in other rooms studyin' about theirselves?"

Kristy says, "Not necessary. Men are already studied in every kind of study. Women have been forced for years to study great men—"

Robert busts in, "Maybe that's the problem, Kristy! Ditch great people. Erase the bastards ... from books and stuff. Just do folks—regular ones—the failures."

Kristy blinks. She touches the soft fabric of her shirt above her heart.

Robert keeps on. "An' wait a minute. Did I get this right, dear? You got men and women studyin' men— great men—in one room, and then women sneak off and study great women in another room and keep the men out?" He pauses for a couple of beats but doesn't really wait for a reply. "When is it they all hang out together and hear about all the stuff together? Or at least all the stuff separately? How come men don't get to hear about great women, big women ... god women, or whatever?"

This is starting to feel like an about to be badly lost chess game to Kristy. "Well, Robert ... we're not at that stage yet. We discourage men from attending many of our classes because it will keep women from being honest about themselves and—"

"I hate to say it, Kristy ..." He is chuckling now. And shaking his head. "I don't mean anything by this ... No offense, dear. But this feminist thing is even worse than I thought. It's really stupid." He wags his head, crosses his eyes.

Kristy looks away from his goofy face to her knee. Then back at his face, his happy red-eyed stoned face. And thanks to the gentling effects of grass, no fight breaks out.

35

TURNING TO A COLD, dark late-day rain outside. While inside the downstairs ell kitchen of the Creighton home, three men talk, two with their forearms on the table, one leaning against the refrigerator with his arms folded: Art and Robert and Mark. With Connie pushing around Mark a half-dozen times to fetch butter, cheeses, eggs, and ginger root. Art has a cup of milky coffee. His short gray hair has its surly little cowlick over the left ear. There are two spots of soft light from the somewhat-authentic 1770s chimney lamps. Connie has all the little ruffled ties off and the curtains drawn. She is starting to feel very paranoid these days about uncovered windows even those that don't show from the street. Bunches of basil, mint, dill, and sage are drying from the open beams. Wilting basil makes such a sour odor.

The men have covered a lot of matters, the Red Sox, stock cars, movies, memorable blizzards, funny stories about septic tanks and septic tank trucks, which then take the conversation to terrible accidents involving tractor trailors and then how it is that overtired truck drivers get made the bad guys by lawmakers and the media but you never hear how taxes and permits, fees, insurance—especially insurance—and maintenance and bloated loans make it so you have to drive for fourteen hours or go down. This gets the conversation onto the speeding up of all of America in everything, especially the pace of work, and by now Robert's voice has grown ugly, and Connie turns from her cutting board and sees the back of his head and neck, the collar of his dark work shirt, his good hand chopping up and down slowly on the table in the same way her knife is crunching down through gingerroot.

She tries to catch Art's eyes to give him a worried look, but both Art and Mark are looking at Robert. They are both with Robert. And now Art speaks and his voice is ugly, too. And Connie pivots around, back to her cutting board and feels this way that they are, at her back with their shared rage, and Mark pulls off his glasses and rubs his eyes so that his eyes, a nice blue, are surrounded in rubbed red, and says something about how if you had yourself an army, a good big army, and you had it out with the government's army that your goal wouldn't be to kill but to wound as many as possible because when you wound one, you are really taking out five or six, all those that stop to help out the wounded guy. And then he says a kind of hotshot thing about nobody stopping him from having a full automatic if he wanted one. "Let 'em try."

And then Robert is talking about his son, Josh, who is eighteen, who has a computer that the school pestered the parents to get. Some deal with a big company through the school. Since the computer arrived, Josh never does anything with Robert, never even looks at his father, because his face is always stuck to his computer ... which also ties up the phone line, which means customers can't get through and so Robert gets pissy and yells at Josh . . . who just ignores him . . . which makes Robert even madder, and now that Cindy works all her different jobs that have different hours than his jobs, there's no supper together anymore, no Sunday dinner, no time to sit across the table from your boy, and therefore Josh is no longer his boy. Josh is theirs, just the way they like it . . . the school, the companies "an' all those other fuckers," and Robert's voice gets really low, which seems to set off his cough.

He hacks deeply, pushing his chair back and coughing down with his head almost between his knees, and Connie sees he presses the knuckles of his good hand into his groin, the hernia most likely, and then when he's back on track, he's railing again, and he tells about how with small business loans at the bank in his town, they can grab your mortgaged property even if you are making your payments, but they have written into your contract in teeny print that if you aren't turning a profit, one they feel is a good one, your business is considered a failure and they have the right to take your mortgaged property just like that! He names three men he knows who this happened to. Each name is spoken with reverence. "Jim Lamb. Bob Champaign. Bob Cousins." And then Robert's voice screams, "SQUEEEEEZED!" And Connie hears an odd sound as she is turning in fright and sees the fist of his strong left hand raised out over the table with a pinkish red matter and liquid rivuleting down his wrist and forearm. It plops on the table.

Art and Mark laugh. Ugly laughs.

It is fruit from the bowl of fruits Connie had set out

for them to snack on. She feels, yes, violated. And hurt. And tight. And breathless.

And then Art, staring meaningfully into Robert's eyes, says deeply, almost in a whisper, "Fuck 'em all." This isn't anything like the Art Connie has known all these years, good wholesome Art, but some other person, who is, like Robert, capable of the unspeakable?

She says, "Art?"

He looks up at her across Robert's shoulder, his gray eyes still caught up in the thing, squinty. And his top lip tight against his teeth. "Yes?"

36

H E RARELY SLEEPS NIGHTS. Almost never undresses, unless he's had a little too much grass. Then he will. And feels cradled by the sweet softly lighted generosity of this place, its strong old smell, and the little dog who curls up with him, his buddy. And he will sleep. And he will dream.

But usually he sits on his bed. Fully dressed. Ready. He eats less and less. He is getting thinner. Lean. Ready.

Sometimes stands at a gable window, curtain pulled to the side, watching through the trees, over the neighbor's roof, that dark awful glow of Boston, a light that breathes.

So now he goes to his bed, sits on the edge of it, smoking a cigarette, knees apart, a tuna fish can ashtray between his sneakered feet.

Tears. No one sees them. So therefore, they do not exist.

No crying, no quivering of the mouth. Just tears of grief. Or terror. Grief. Terror. Sometimes grief. Sometimes terror. And shame. But no regret. No regret. No regret.

37

BEFORE SUPPER, Connie is sitting sideways on a chair at the partially set dining-room table. She hears Robert coughing in the back hall. Then he appears in the doorway there, his hair wet from a shower, Duane trotting along even with his steps as he enters the room.

Duane hops onto a chair at the table, under the table actually, worms his head up through the space between the chair back and table edge, looks up at Connie.

Robert coughing again croakily. He crosses the soft rugs over to Connie, sees first that her face is stony, then sees under her hand, on the table, his own face. The *Washington Post* . . . front page . . . his face and the accompanying print filling the whole bottom half. More details about the assassination, old details rehashed, new details dredged up, lest America be anything less than faithfully riveted.

Connie says not one word.

He says a little too breezily, "Don't read that shit."

"I need to," she explains in her deepest, darkest, saddest voice. "I need to know *everything.*"

He glances around the floor, across one stretch of mopboard as if for something lost.

She says, "You don't tell us everything so we need to go elsewhere." She pats the paper.

"Sure," he says quietly, shrugs.

"Your rage, Robert, it—"

He says too quickly, "Ain't nuthin' you ever wanna see."

"Who has seen it besides the people at the Parker House?"

He stares at her.

"You ever hit Cindy?"

"I do not hit women."

"Your kids?"

"I do not hit kids. I spank them."

"In a rage?"

He squints. Muscles all over him are tightening. He says quietly, "I don't like this. I want you to stop. Now."

"Don't tell me to stop! I want you to stop! You will not terrorize me in my own home!"

She stands up, lifts the paper high with the picture of his face, enlarged from a cheap camera photo and therefore softened, a picture he does not remember being taken, thereby giving him a real creepy sensation, like with senility when whole chunks of your life float in forgotten space, a photo of himself as he looks this moment—the hard mouth, the long moustache, the short beard, bit of gray—this version of his face held by Connie's trembling hand at the same height as his own living face...and he looks across at it and quickly away, and Connie almost sobs these words, "There is no need for anger to go this far!"

His jaws clench. He swallows. "Like I say, it's nuthin' you ever want to see."

Connie balls up this section of the paper and another . . . violently. Two fat firm grayish ball shapes. She slings them overhand. Both hit him. One bounces off his face. She hollers, "He was shivering! And whimpering!"

Robert, having blinked when the paper shapes hit him, has not moved, now just stares at her agonized face, her trembling chin. Then he says, "Yes, he was."

38

TELEVISIONS ACROSS America in their perpetual effervescence, telling how authorities are confident that Robert Drummond will be in custody before long, that there are new leads.

In actuality, agents are gritting their teeth and cracking their knuckles and making funny little neck sounds over the old blood reports and recent questionings all seeming to dead-end. And one guy grumbles, "Where the fuck is he?"

39

THE SENATOR'S WIFE is not a conservative dresser like her daughter. Constance Creighton's nighttime dreams are in polka dots and flowers. She thinks in color, like some people think in English or Swahili. It is with great restraint, it is with pain, that she tones down her wardrobe for her husband's political career, whenever she is seen with him or for those appearances she makes as the "senator's wife." For him, this small sacrifice. To be or not to be the true Connie! Political persons, like top management of the great businesses, one and the same, like the priests of old, chiseled expressionless conduit of the great benign but stern gods, or God—or as it is today, not God, but the system: "the Great Society," "the Progressive Society," the ladder of opportunity. AMERICA!

Who is the real Connie? For a time she had wished she were black. Odetta. Breathtakingly tribal. Feet wide apart. A voice as big as a temple. There are many shops in Boston that cater to Connie's tastes, imported gauzy cottons, rayons, fabrics like sunsets, dragon greens, Pharaoh golds. Though the real full-blown Connie is nothing you can find in a shop. With a sewing machine, Connie used to create herself. She was her own masterpiece. Her own sculpture. A walking installation. If she could have made sandals and sneakers, *wunderbar!* As it is, her sneaker collection is quite the spectacle. Polka dots, yes. Little jungle animals. A multitude of colors. She has seen camo sneakers but wrinkled her nose. Camo? Not quite. What about jewelry? She hates to have anything around her neck or wrists. She never had her ears pierced. Oh gawd, no, ugh! The wedding band and diamond she has gotten used to. For him. Meanwhile, she has photos of African women around her sunporch studio, swathed in yards of fertile color, celebration color. Forget the nose rings, neck stretchers, and long ears. But the color! If only Capitol Hill dressed like this!

This morning she enters the downstairs library, a lovely room of orangy pine floors and small rugs, but not much light. All those rare books! Light fades things. And now keeping out the eyes of the law. The whole house has become like a cave. But in some ways this library makes a light of its own. A few deep chairs. Hundreds of book spines, their titles, the bricks of civilization. A well-camouflaged stereo and barely noticeable speakers. Records, tapes, CDs. Bach and Mozart down through some of that contemporary toneless stuff. Connie has many composer friends. Oh, and by the way, Jerry was not one of those who tried to kill the NEA, just tone it down some. Institutions of art can handle grants better than individuals can anyway, he said. And besides, "It is the political climate."

As her eyes get accustomed to the almost-sepia library dimness, she sees over by one window, with the drapes pinned over to one side with a heavy book on the sill, Robert.

He is sitting hunched over on a short-legged backless stool with Duane devotedly at his feet, and he is looking down at something in his lap.

Though the spruce trees are thick beyond, she tugs the drape a bit to make a smaller opening, painfully nervous of them, irritated at him for not being so careful.

She is wearing sneakers of the ultimate yellow, a kind of OSHA yellow, which make her feet look as huge as her feet were in Robert's drawing of her.

She sees on his lap, one of her books, the first one she had published. The turtle book. He looks up. "This book . . . we have this at home. You are famous, huh?"

"Well, so-so. Fame these days has more to do with film, books that translate into film . . . so you get groupies. Like your Stephen King. Children's literature doesn't get made into film much, therefore—"

"What about *Lassie?*"

She smiles indulgently.

"And the *Wizard of Oz?*" He looks down at Duane, who flattens and perks his ears.

"Well, those are rare instances . . . not to mention ancient."

He stands. He looks good today. Though perhaps a little thinner. Eyes getting a bit of a deep look. He doesn't eat. He doesn't look like a nervous wreck. But. He. Must. Be. Meanwhile, the fevers have subsided. He wears the red T-shirt Kristy got him. That red with his black hair. Pink plaid sling. And all those tattoos. Connie breathes deep, then almost sorrowfully says, "I loved your drawing of me."

He flushes. Dismisses it. "That was nothing. I'm shitty at art."

"I disagree. I say you are gifted."

"You flatterer." He pokes her arm, the way kids poke each other to start a wrassle.

Duane watches this, the voices going back and forth, the smiles and grimaces, the little play poke.

Connie insists that Robert has the gift.

Robert shifts his weight, feet apart, shrugging his shoulders, now with the turtle book in one hand, working the pages in a way that shows he is getting quite good at being one-handed. He says something, mumbling in his strong White Mountains foothills accent. She doesn't hear it. She has been taken by one of her creative flashes. A vision of Robert as artist: *He leads all of America's starving artists in their true NEA revenge. Instead of camo and militia patches, the artists would wear berets and smocks. The writers would wear tweed jackets with leather elbow patches, even the women. All armed. With swords. Not guns. And Robert would ride a snorting restless gray stallion to lead the greatly talented indignant hordes to the Parker House. And once inside, instead of all that "fucker" stuff, they would scream out great lines of Dylan Thomas and Ezra Pound.*

Robert is looking at her in a strange way.

She realizes she has been looking zoned out, probably staring with her mouth open or something. She sees he still has her book in his hand.

How can this be? How can one day she see the ruin he has left of other lives, seeing that hand, ringless and shapely, capable of executing a crying man ... then today with every bright nerve of her being, be so lighthearted, so full of fun, so adoring? Is this what the junction of Robert Drummond's life with hers has come to teach her? That she is this easily devitalized and wishy-washy? Yeah, so principles come to nothing. Right and wrong is nothing. So what is to keep this world from flying apart?

40

IN THE NIGHT he is up after a surprisingly deep, untroubled sleep, shuts the study room's French doors, walks the rooms of glowing dormers—glowing with pink outside security lights, microwave, funny phones— to the bathroom, flicks on the switch, doesn't shut the door, just stands sleepily pissing into the toilet, which he calls "the flush" though sometimes he forgets to flush it. A lot of piss tonight. It kind of thunders. So when he hears a pained sound, like two mice fighting, maybe two rats, behind him, he is startled, even before he shakes himself dry, turning with wide eyes. Kristy.

Kristy sees that he is as nude as when she didn't know him, when he was only a body on the bed, with no vitality, no tenderness, no aggravating habits and wrong things said.

He sees that she wears a long wine-colored robe with a monogrammed KRC over one breast. She looks upset, not happy to see him here, and all in about three beats from his turning, still hanging on to himself, to shake it, she pushes hard at his arm, the arm that hangs at his side, the shoulder that, without its gauze, looks like a contour map of a ruggedly mountainous country. The shoulder. It always hurts. But it is a bigger hurt when jarred. And she covers her face with both hands, as he has seen her do before, and she hops, like in a tantrum, and gasps, "No more! No more!"

And this is all very fast in only that same few moments following his turning from "the flush," still unflushed, and he is thinking of asking, "No more what?" but just looks at her face as she draws her hands down. He just looks at her face, not angrily, but perceptively. No longer bewildered by Kristy Creighton. He now knows what ticks. He hears Duane digging at the closed study-room doors. Probably about to rip a rug in half next.

He reaches for Kristy's short glossy hair, the thickness of it at the back of her head, and gripping this hair hard, draws her head down and he says, "Suck it, Ms."

And she just, yes, does it ... but only after first licking him clean. Kristina Creighton, a true animal. She squats a bit, almost as low as the senator in the lobby of the Parker House, then, yes, down, just that low, licking and licking back across the bristliness of his scrotum then farther on to the tender rectum, washing, washing like an unfalteringly tender mother of beasts, one that never never never questions that tenderness is really strength, that giving is supreme.

And all the while he grips with one hand the edge of the open door frame, kind of losing consciousness to the feel of this, till she stops. Then he pulls her to her feet and smiles. She is whispering to herself, eyes closed, her mouth chafed bright. Her whispers are like prayers. When she opens her eyes, she sees he is standing there looking at her with one eye squinted, in something like disbelief, and then he says, "Take off the robe, Kristy."

She opens the robe, pulls it off her shoulders. Just white ordinary panties. Bare breasts. High, cone shaped. Nipples dark, gone soft in the heat.

He nods to the white panties. "Take them off."

She pulls them down fast with her eyes shut, whispering to herself again, raising each leg, struggling the slippery fabric over each ankle, opening her eyes to see that seductive hard-assed look, that very wrong look that precedes every wolf whistle, every politically incorrect degrading-to-women word and thought, his eyes sliding up from where she just jerked the panties free from her left bare foot, eyes moving up her legs over her darkly haired "cunt"—yes, that would be his word—up, up, up to her eyes, her eyes, which just can't seem to hold his stare, but she sees that little suggestive swing of his thick shoulders and he hollers, "Down! Down, Ms. Bitch Bad-Loser Bitch! Sit!"

And she actually does this almost before he is done with this command, her panties still in one hand. And the bathroom tiles are warm, all the heat of two lower floors giving them life against her bottom and her back and to his knees as he, in this game where winners and losers both win, is now returning the gift of humility ... with teeth and tongue. Isn't it this, instead of *an eye for an eye, a tooth for a tooth*, isn't it true that humility for humility brings rightness? The right thing.

And she closes her eyes, whispers to herself as he desperately finds his position. And then he is ramming and ramming, and Kristy can't remember any of her opinions, any of her principles before Robert Drummond showed up here. She can't remember any of her "education." None of that applies in this territory. The talking heads roll into their quiet corners.

Afterward, she leads him to her bedroom, though he is worried about Duane being alone, so Duane joins them. The bed is full sized. The room is hot. No open windows here to let the heat out, nor to dilute the scent of sweet talcs and fresh fabrics. In the dark, Kristy and Robert talk about childhood, and it seems they both had wonderful childhoods, though Robert tells her nothing about school, and then he asks for his gun back and she gives it to him.

IN THE MORNING before light, she is wakened by his leaving the bed, leaving the room. And Duane scuttling after him. The hinges and the doorknob whisper. The hall floor creaks. She flips over onto her back, eyes wide. "Jesus. Jesus, Jesus," she whispers sorrowfully.

42

L ATER, SAME DAY. Another weird tropical day brings a grumble of thunder across the distances, marching closer and closer. Robert is alone in the house. Connie has taken Duane to the vet—Duane's vet, not Robert's vet. Skin trouble. Allergies. Miseries. And Kristy? Somewhere.

He watches TV, the TV turned low. Sees himself in the news. Sees they believe he still could be in the Boston area. Sees how the newly, hurriedly doctored-up federal antiterrorism laws have provided for his death. By hanging. In spite of the screams of Amnesty International and every other human rights group. A lot of gun stuff and spying stuff and shorten-the-appeals stuff and all manner of terrorist-exceptions-to-the-Bill-of-Rights stuff working its way up from Congress to the president's plain pink hand quickie-quick, yeah, fast as a flushing toilet.

The thunder booms closer now.

No gun oil here. He considers looking for some 10-W-40 down in the Stable. He goes to a window, plucks the curtain aside with a finger, sees the government car at the end of the street. Has his gun stuffed in his belt.

He thinks of Gina. His youngest sister. He never knew her while they were growing up, she being so much younger and so quiet. Now she's Gina Libby. Widow. He can see her clearly: Dark haired. Sweet dresser. Nervous smoker. Married Kevan. Kevan and Ruff thick as thieves. They worked together in the woods. Worked together well. They agreed on everything. They agreed that a few senators had to die.

Robert knows Gina is hurting bad. She and Kevan were fighting when Kevan left with the others for Boston in two separate trucks. No one knew where they were going. Gina probably thought she and Kevan would make up by supper time. Sure, she thought that.

Ruff and Kevan and the others knew a lot about certain senators. Though not enough. They had the big picture, oh yes. But the details. So many fucking details like warts on a toad. Therefore, ordinary people gotta simplify.

He steps away from the window, curtain drops back in place. With his feet apart and the hammer on an empty chamber, five shells ready, he "practices" with his old single-action Blackhawk. No, not exactly a military gun. More of a Matt Dillon gun. He aims it at Kristy's computer between the farther two backside dormers, then tries to sight in on Paris, depicted as a lusty-looking red dot on the map of France, which is framed and hangs quite cleverly on the slanted wall/ceiling.

He pretends to pull the trigger just as the thunder is blamming and crackling, echoing between buildings, the trees tossing, rain hissing outside the open windows, wetting down the south-side sills now, the rain really letting go now. And the lightning is like uncountable flashbulbs of uncountable cameras going off as he is being led by them to the gallows. Oh boy.

He can't believe it, how far down a hole America has gone since his happy childhood. How Wild Westish things seem now. Or maybe, Bible-ish. But the great pyramids being built by the enslaved people today aren't stone. They are plastic.

He knows federal agent fuckers and media fuckers are swarming like carrion beetles all over his Cindy, his kids, Gina and her kids, all his brothers and sisters, the whole fuckin' town.

He clenches his jaws. He goes to the window again, pulls the curtain aside, wide. A brightness falls across the room. Now as the lightning rips down through the purpling sky, seeming only yards away, he sees Kristy's Porsche edging up to the gates and sees her face through the flip-flop of the wipers, looking up at him and again, too quickly, one great show of light and a crackly deep-boned BOOM!, and he waves to Kristy and makes a funny face. She doesn't wave back.

43

WHEN THE STORM recedes, there's a pale coolness at the skylights, all the goldenness and normalness of October. And from a crinkly bookstore bag, Kristy lays a thickness of friendship cards and thank-you cards on the kitchenette table, and artsy postcards, and five new books, their covers thin and glossy and cheesy and ready to curl, the way all soft-cover books are these days.

His footsteps sound different. Causes her to look around fast. Looking first at his face, then his feet. In the daylight, in the harder considerations of daytime, everything is regret. She sighs.

He is wearing, not his sneakers, but old work boots. Yes, old work boots. Like the ones she had pulled off his feet and threw away. But these are not bloody. Probably a present from Art. She can usually tell when Art and Mark have been up here for a visit. Robert acts different, straighter shouldered and . . . something. Though getting his gun back probably also makes him walk differently. She asks nothing. She just reddens, then goes back to fussing with her new books.

And he reddens. Though she doesn't see that he does. She pulls another book from the bag.

He says, "I'm sorry."

"About what?" she says quickly.

"Weirdness."

"Which weirdness?" She flips through the book. "You mean standing in the window and drawing attention to yourself? Or . . . last night?"

"All of it. I apologize for all shit."

She shrugs.

He laughs nervously. "Kristy. Last night was good." He reaches up and traces the refrigerator company's name on the freezer door. "It was." He looks at her with his expression a little bit too much like that cocky look he had last night in the bathroom.

"But weird," she says darkly.

He laughs. "Oral sex isn't weird."

"I don't mean that." With a tight insincere smile and closed eyes, she asks, "OK, Mr. Right Wing, Mr. Big-Shot Right Wing. You say all that big-man stuff to your wife? Get down and suck? Take this off? Take that off?"

She opens her eyes because he's not answering, sees that he's looking hard at her, shaking his head slowly, significantly . . . not as a no, but the way you shake your head to pity a pathetic person.

She laughs again, a very tight laugh. "Well?"

He looks sheepish now, an actual blush, turns to the refrigerator, in fact faces it squarely, places the toe of his work boot against the plastic bottom.

She whispers, "I don't get it. Why don't I get it?"

He looks around at her and squints. He snorts a little

bit happily. "You're just like your mum. Big Question ladies."

Her eyes fill with tears.

He looks alarmed. "Don't, baby," he says, and puts a hand out.

She puts her hand out, too, and he grasps two of her fingers, and her chin puckers and tears flood brightly down to the corners of her mouth.

He says, "Jesus." And hugs her to him with his good arm. "It was just playing."

Against his neck, his collar, his solidness, she says, "But I liked it. I *liked* it!"

"Jesus. Stop it!" He laughs nervously. "Don't think about it. It was just playin' around. Made us feel good. So what? Nuthin' sick about it."

"But you don't get it, do you, Robert!" she says with a snivelly laugh. "I lost my mind."

"You're supposed to lose your mind, dear. Nobody fucks usin' their thoughts." He squashes his mouth to her ear, gives her a wet, hurtingly loud smooch.

She jerks away. Holds her ear. "Don't do stuff like that!" she shrieks.

He closes a tough, work-thickened hand around one of her wrists, and he makes a funny face like a snarling bear.

She smiles a little. With one finger, she delicately wipes each eye.

He says, "Next time you think you're sick 'cause you and some guy like to play rough, have a good talk with a chicken."

"A what?"

"A chicken." He blinks both of his eyes. "Every

mornin' before a rooster fucks some hens, he chases 'em around. The hens run around and squawk. But then they squat down. They want it but they wanna run around a little first and pretend stuff. Makes their blood fast...all that runnin' and squawkin' and pretendin'. Millions of chickens do this. *Millions*."

She turns away, goes back to the table, pulls another book from the bag and then speaks with a voice of bitter sadness, "I love you."

He says, "I love you back."

"Don't stand in the window again. Not ever. Never. Never. Never."

He looks up at the skylights. Sky a painful blue. He looks back into Kristy's eyes. Very blue. "I have to go, Kristy. Soon. I can't stay. I gotta get it over with, you know. Either shit or get off the pot. Right?"

No reply.

"You hear me?"

"Yes, sir. I hear you."

"Soon."

"Soon." Her tears have stopped. Her face is stony.

ND SHE TELLS HER mother everything. Everything.
She has never felt so intimate with Connie before.
She even wants Connie to have a sense of humor
about it. She hopes Connie will have something hi-
larious to say about the chickens. But Connie's eyes
are especially round and on toward a dark shade of
gray. Connie doesn't even ask questions. She just listens
to all the woman-to-woman details with her mouth a
compressed line. And Kristy says, "Oh, Mom. I'm so
afraid. Isn't there some way we can get him out of the
country?"

Connie's eyes widen more.

Kristy says quickly, "Oh, I know . . . he'd never be
happy in another country . . . He might as well be . . .
be . . . whatever happens . . ." She stops talking. She sees
that her mother is giving her a look on each and every
word as though each and every word was the stupidest
thing anyone ever said.

The hair stands up on Kristy's arms and the back of

her neck. Her own eyes widen now and the silence is like cold sea and cold stone.

And then Connie says in a sugary voice, "Everything will work out . . . for you. Ten years from now you will have learned from this."

45

HE LIES ON HIS BED, fully dressed, gun in his belt, the taste of supper in his teeth, thinking about his Cindy, her smells, that fond torrent of smells one body can give you over twenty good-lovin' years, and the smells of home—of the house, the trees, the sky—which are actually the same as the smells of his wife. And the couch where they sleep, folding it out every night, the sound of that couch being folded out. Don't cry, Cindy. You don't know Kristy Creighton. In a dreamy way, he sees his wife's face begin to speak, then the face and head shrink tiny as a cat's, mouth and eyes contorting into some creaturely anguish. Her shrinking body jerks like in a brain fit. He sits up fast, his neck cords squeezing. He presses a palm to his forehead, eyes wide, blinking. Cindy Mindy Squindy. See, I am dead. Forget me. Kristy, too. Soon you, too, gotta forget this dumb fuck. Everyone stop crying!

46

FTER THE million-dollar reward is offered for information leading to the capture and conviction of Robert Drummond, TVs all over America tell with good humor of how Drummond was seen in Florida, in L.A., in a Chicago suburb, Kentucky, and at a Canadian–Washington State border crossing ... all on the same day. An FBI spokesman humorlessly explains into a thicket of mikes that none of these reports was confirmed, that the agency still believes Drummond is hiding in the Boston area. There is absolutely no evidence to the contrary.

ONNIE COMES slamming into the house in her long olive-colored, imitation mink–collared coat, leather shoulder bag, a kind of windswept look to her sandy hair. She flomps the leather bag onto the high-backed entryway bench, pulls out papers, listens for the direction of Duane's welcoming bark. Upstairs.

She hurries up the stairs, coat flapping, finds the apartment horribly hot again, the way Kristy likes it, and she finds Robert in Kristy's little living room, shirtless, inside a significantly stinky fog of cigarette smoke, Duane greeting her happily, and Kristy at her kitchenette table, barefoot, baggy jersey and jeans, looking up from texts, her doctoral dissertation paperwork piled around her. She smiles at her mother guiltily. And Robert, no cigarette in sight, stands up, no sling, working the hand of his damaged arm with his fingers, opening them but not tightening them, and there is all this wild color of his arms, and Connie points at him and commands, "Sit down!" And he does, slowly. And she tosses her handful of papers into his lap.

Kristy comes toward her and says, "What's up, Mom? How are Jenny and Phyllis?"

Connie keeps her eyes on Robert's face as he looks down at the copied materials, mostly articles from leftist journals and recent dissident newsletters. She says, "Jenny and Phyllis are just dandy."

Robert looks long and hard at a picture that heads one article.

Kristy says, "Whatcha got there, Robert?"

Connie says, "Well, Robert. This leads me to the question. What *are* you? I've been led to believe you are right wing."

Robert rolls the papers up tight in his good hand. "I ain't no wing," he says humorlessly. Then he looks up at Kristy.

Kristy asks again, "What are those, Robert?"

Connie explains, "His heroes. The MRTA in Peru ... Tupac Amuru Revolutionary Movement's Nestor Cerpa ... tortured and murdered by, in essence, the New World Order, and the Zapatistas of Chiapas in Mexico ... their subcomandante Marcos, still alive as far as we know but sticking his neck wayyyyy out on the chopping block these days. Robert, these guys are leftists!"

Robert stands up fast, sneers. "It ain't left or right. It's up and down. You're either up or you're down. That's all there is to it. OK?"

Connie narrows her eyes. "Could you be a little clearer, Mr. Drummond?"

Robert frowns.

Kristy says, "He means either you are a financier up there. Or you are a Mayan or a ... Mainer *way* down in the pits."

Connie asks, "How many lefty militias *are* there in this country? This is really shocking."

Robert looks like he has just swallowed something that tastes awful. His mustache trembles.

Kristy says, "Mom, it's not left or right for most people. It's just a big mess." She looks at Robert. "Mom would love to think you are a lefty."

Robert has nothing to say. Just continues to look as if he's been forced to swallow something very pale and treacherous.

Kristy wonders softly, "Mom, if he were left, would it make it OK . . . you know . . . would it make what he did all right?"

Connie speaks in her most throaty and yet most booming voice, "It is best not to think! Thinking leads to tangles and bitter regret!" And she turns to go downstairs to hang her coat up and make a nice big fat drink.

48

IT IS NOW WELL INTO November. Trees bare. Close-treed lawns of the neighborhood burned gray by glistening frost, the sun looking somehow both larger and smaller, bearing in sideways on brick and stone and handsome front doors with big brass knockers and statice wreathes or Indian corn and on shrubberies perfectly shaped as pieces of furniture.

Connie Creighton doesn't like to drink in the morning, but somehow drinks have been finding her hand at all times of the day lately. Nothing powerful. Just tasty. Just piña coladas. Thick.

She should be getting showered and dressed instead of flomping around in this robe. She has a Women's Peace Action luncheon to attend, has to be met by certain VIPs an hour earlier. The toned-down navy-blue-suit Constance Creighton la la la. And two FBI men whom she has agreed to let "accompany" her there. All morning she has gotten too lost in the Russian novel. All those tissuey pages and eensy print. Another twenty pages of a Russian nobleman's inner angst over with. Now back to the war. She carries the drink back down the hall toward the library, where she has left the book open in a deep chair, raises the latch, and there is Robert at a window, back pressed to the frame, the drapes bunched behind one shoulder, face stony, gun pointed at her.

She makes a deep sound, ugly, cowlike.

He quickly lowers the gun. He whispers, "There's somebody tryin' to get in here...somebody..."—he jerks his head toward the window—"out there...I heard them crackling in those bushes." He again tips his head at the window but keeps his eyes on her.

"Cat," she says, her face as stony as his, but her eyes on the gun, now held low against the side of his thigh.

He says, "Maybe a cat. Maybe not."

Duane is standing alertly at Robert's feet, head turned toward the window.

Connie sees the camo shirt with its Snow Men patch, the sleeves rolled up tight over his elbows, no sling. The bad arm hangs at his side. This shirt is what he has told her he will wear when he leaves. He wants to die in this shirt, like the rest of his militia. He can't stay here forever. But each day passes and he is still here. And they are still out there. And Connie lifts the drink to her lips, sips it, her hand just a twinge shaky from her scare. She says, "This house is going to self-destruct...soon, isn't it, Robert? Can you feel it? Us—all of us—with little bombs inside us?" She takes a big fat swallow of her drink.

He works the hammer and cylinder of his revolver deftly—click, click, click, click, click—lowers the hammer easy, stuffs the gun in his belt outside his shirt. He looks around the room, everywhere but her face. He looks truly cornered. He asks, "When is your husband gettin' here for . . . that visit?"

"He's been detained. He's in Iran."

"Iran?" He scrinches his face the way he had at "AIDS" and "good grades in school."

She assures him, "Don't worry. Jerry won't come home without calling. We have to be prepared. He had hoped to just sneak back here for a little rest. But now he has a few people who want to see him here. No rest for the weary. He has to fit everything in. Starts when he comes in the door."

Robert is watching her mouth, his chin raised like a soldier's at attention.

"You know . . . there's something else." She lowers her drink to the stand beside her reading chair. "It's . . . that he has been advised not to come to Boston until . . . you are in custody . . . caught . . . locked up. They suspect you are still in Boston."

He doesn't smile, though she is kind of smiling. He just backs up to the window again and picks up the edge of the drape and looks down into the shrubberies that are against the house. Then he looks back at her and he smiles with his eyes. "I thank you for puttin' up with me. You and Kristy are sweet people. You an' her aren't like the rest."

Kristy has stopped telling her things . . . about Robert. But she knows they carry on upstairs routinely. She can see it in Kristy's eyes. She has seen a hickey on Kristy's neck. She swears she smells sex in every room of Kristy's apartment when she's up there. She stares at a row of books over the louvers that hide a TV screen, then lowers her eyes, closes her eyes.

"You OK, Connie?"

She bursts into tears. A real hammering sob. Covers her face.

"Hey!" He goes over to her and Duane rushes at her, bouncing with all four feet off the front of her robe, and Robert hugs her head to him, a kind of wrassly, fatherly hug. He says, "Everybody's falling apart 'cause of this shit. I'm tryin' to get outa here...I'm just workin' up the fuckin' courage. Don't worry. It'll come to me. I just need a kick in the ass. Tell me to get the fuck out. I'll go if you—"

"No! Don't leave!" She gets a crushing grip on his hand. Kisses his hand. Tears and crying-mouth drool wetting his hand.

His eyes widen and darken. He hugs her, twirls her a little. Like a dance. "You are beautiful."

She makes no reply. Her face is mashed against his shirt. She just breathes.

"I said you are beautiful," he repeats, nuzzles the top of her head.

She sobs, "No! No, I'm not. I'm old and flumpy!"

"None of us is getting any younger," he reminds her.

No reply. Just a kind of squeaky moan against his shirt.

He thrusts his left work boot between her slippered feet. "You got some place you wanna lay down with me?" he asks.

Her face pressed into his shirt laughs, then breathes again, one deep, slow drag, like taking in a good-feeling drug.

"Huh?" he presses. "Huh? You gonna answer me?"

Now in the master bedroom on the second floor, Duane slips in around their feet and is the first on the big bed, bouncing around, panting happily, yapping. Duane watches the robe drop to the floor. Duane observes Robert placing his revolver on the nightstand. Duane sees it all. There in the center of the senator's big bed, Connie naked on her back, Robert Drummond, uniform shirt still buttoned to the throat, just unbuckles his belt, unzips his jeans, tugging out that long, thick pecker that Kristy had, after that night in the bathroom, described to her mother in splendorous detail, and with a deep appreciative groan, he puts it to the senator's wife.

WHILE SOMEWHERE out in the city, Kristy has lunch with two old friends, one of whom is in love with his computer, talks the language, knows its soul, has even given it a beautiful name: Helen.

MEANWHILE, only two blocks away from the Creighton home, the FBI has a little talk with another neighbor about what she saw on the evening after Senator Davies's assassination. And the FBI guys' eyes brighten as they nod and listen.

AND MEANWHILE, in Washington, Jerry Creighton, just back from Iran only an hour ago, smiles at the lobbyist from Archer Daniels who has just said such a witty thing about D.C. water and corn syrup.

AND MEANWHILE, the senator's wife wraps her legs around Robert Drummond, shrieks and yeowls like a witch.

Does Robert Drummond understand this triumph? That maybe to Senator Jerry Creighton some things could be worse than death?

49

ROUND 4:30 THAT afternoon, a call. Again it's the deep-voiced FBI man. His name is Tim Jacques. He is both kindly and pushy. He insists that Connie accept a couple of "security personnel" on her property. He tells her that the FBI now has four corroborated witnesses from her neighborhood who on the evening after the assassination saw a man of Drummond's description walking in a hunched, injured manner toward her street. He tells her that it was only another two blocks away that the agents tested samples of blood from the sidewalk a few hours after the incident, blood that, it turns out, matches Drummond's blood type.

Connie still refuses the protection, seems so very cavalier.

The deep-voiced Tim Jacques after a long, astute silence explains that her husband would really like it if she accepted the protection. Then, seeing this has no effect, gives up. With a polite thank you, he is gone.

Now Connie sits in the big kitchen of weedy, drying herb smells and simmering soup, her palms firmly one to each eye, listening to distant after-work traffic. She hears Duane yapping upstairs. Probably Robert teasing and play-ing with him, doing "ugly bear versus ugly wolf." How long can this restless, vivid man be kept secret inside these walls? She grieves. He is still alive on her skin, even inside the dark pathway to her someday-soon-to-be-forgotten womb, yet she grieves for the loss of him. And when the phone rings, she cries out. She stands up fast but is slow to put the phone to her ear. Jerry. He is calling to tell her he would feel better if the FBI could do its job. This looks bad . . . for him. He questions her obstinacy.

She speaks close to the receiver in a small, strange way, clearly not obstinacy, but desperation. "Please, Jerry, no."

He adds that the FBI needs to interview her. They are canvassing the whole neighborhood, and so far everyone has been eager to help.

She makes no comment.

He asks, "Don't you want to help them find the guy who blasted Kip Davies's brains out?" He is on to her in some way. In some way he knows? In some way he at least knows she is in some other program. On another team. Supporting another policy. Some little coup d'état?

50

ANOTHER NOVEMBER day. Frosty. The light is a mean but pure thing. Art and Mark are painting window screens in the Stable. The paint is a rich tile green.

Robert appears in the bay, hands in pockets, offers to help. Art's face drains of color. Robert walks casually in among the paint cans and sawhorses, Duane at his heels. Art quietly points out the tray of clean brushes, a can opener, cans of new paint stacked.

Robert works with a lighted cigarette in his teeth.

Duane checks everything out, wears green paint on his feet, small green footprints all over the newspapers and old rough gray wooden floors.

Everyone's breath is frosty.

Art hasn't really regained his composure or the color in his face. Not much to say.

Robert coughs, one of those deep strangling kind. A lotta years of smoke.

Mark tells Robert what he's heard around, that a lot of citizens' militias are speaking out—loud and clear—against him. They are purely defense and "don't need another Oklahoma City bombing or this to give 'em a bad name. One or two of 'em say you probably didn't really do it. That you're being framed . . . that probably the government did it . . . to make the Movement look bad. But most of 'em feel you did it. They say they wanna see you hang . . . They all wanna be there . . . This is what they say . . . They want to be there and cheer when you swing from the noose . . . This is what they say . . . And they're calling for a public flogging." Mark shakes his head, laughs nervously. "Jesus."

Robert listens and nods, and drops his cigarette butt, twists the heel of his work boot over it, lights another, the smoke giving one of his eyes a big squint as he dips into the paint, working a beautiful second coat onto a screen frame. He speaks no defense of himself. Shows no alarm. No disappointment.

Art is edgier by the minute. Robert keeps moving back and forth around this wide-open bay. Even with the spruce trees and the curve of the bricked drive, there are several gaps showing the street. Yeah, Robert, he is maybe the kind of guy who could take others down with him? Although maybe it's that Robert sees the Creighton family as above the law, which in some sense is true. But even for the rich, things can turn when it's time for that. There is a time for all things.

Art is starting to chill toward Robert. This is Art's way of protecting himself from pain. Maybe he speaks a little too gruffly today, the few times he speaks. Mostly he just works, breathing hard through his nose, the frostiness streaming from his nose, his nose red, eyes watering.

51

Again in the senator's bed, Robert undressed this time, spends the night with Connie. Neither one sleeps, not even a few minutes of drifting. It is a fierce wrassle, Connie pressing him to play harder, to do his "ugly bear" thing, somehow dangerously bordering on his hard-assed Mr. Right Wing thing that Kristy had described, and Connie has, unlike Kristy, absolutely no trouble playing along ... pressing him to play even harder, which he does.

And then they rest and whisper.

And Connie actually seems happy.

Her fingers rake over his back and she says, "I love your skin. It's like velvet. Not dry like mine and ..." She decides not to speak her husband's name. But in a matter-of-fact voice, "Robert. Can I ask you a question?"

He snorts, face in the pillow. "You always ask questions."

"Yes, I do. But this one ..." She tries to get her long hair twisted into a manageable rope behind her, as there in the dim ivory light of her marble-base floor lamp, she is sitting and he is lying on his stomach half buried in somewhat perfumey sheets. "Robert, why were you in our Stable when we found you? Did you just wander there in a daze? Is it just a big coincidence that this is the home of another senator? Or . . . did you think for some reason you'd find Jerry here and kill him?"

Robert says evenly, "I came to kill him."

Connie drops her hands, letting her hair have its true will, while against her knee, the feel of his bony hip, warm against warm.

"But I won't. Not now." These words muffled, his face partly mashed into his pillow. "It's too close."

"Too close? What do you mean *too close?*"

He turns on his side to face her. "I wouldn't fuck you and Kristy over like that."

She laughs, one deep satisfying guffaw. She sighs. "I can't believe this life."

THE NEXT NIGHT, a tap on the door of the master bedroom. Connie steps through the warm ivory glow made by the dimly lighted marble-base floor lamp. She lifts the latch and Kristy is standing there in her dark robe, her hair messy like a toddler's, her eyes on her mother's face. She steps past her mother into the big room and looks at the bed, stares at it. She says in an ordinary voice, "I came down to talk with you last night...about why Robert might be missing from his bed."

Connie closes the door. Sighs.

Kristy sits on the bed.

Connie says deeply, almost ghoulishly, "He will be gone soon."

Kristy hunches her shoulders, looking down at her hands.

Connie says, again meaningfully deep, "He's not yours. He's not mine. He's not even Mrs. Cindy Drummond's anymore. He belongs to them! He is on his way to them very soon!"

Kristy says wearily, "I didn't come in here to argue that. I'm not mad at you. Just . . . just confused."

Connie tightens her sash, hugs herself. Chortles. "We've all gone nuts."

Kristy says, "I've never loved a man this much."

Connie lays a hand on the cool top of the near dresser.

Kristy wonders, "And you?"

Connie flops her hand to her side. "How can I not love him? He lives and dies *so that man shall live.*"

Through the dimness Kristy sees her mother's hands, her mother's well-spaced bare feet, green aging eyes that look no less sane, no more passionate than ever. Kristy hunches her shoulders again, her slim girlish shoulders. She giggles. "Mom, you always say the funniest things."

Connie quietly asks, "Did you feel that was actually funny?"

Kristy shrugs. She folds her hands in the lap of her robe. Primly. "Mom, I . . . can't imagine . . . him . . . it . . . what he did to Kip Davies. I can't imagine any of it. Not now."

"Mm-hmmm."

"How could he go that far?"

Connie kind of grunts. Shifts her weight to the opposite foot. "You know, it's an old story. Goes way back to . . . you know . . . Og hit Mog with a stick. Is Og a bad man? See the stick split Mog's head. Kinda bad. Yes, it is bad. Peace is best. But is peace in a cage really peace? Is peace on your knees really peace? The definition of peace is . . . I suppose . . . like the definition of space. Og hits Mog with stick. Kristy, that's just a little bitty scene from a long, long story, a great epic of transgressions and cruelties upon the tribe of Og. Is it really virtuous to lie down in peace when your people are being assaulted, heart, body, and soul?" She walks heavily to the bed and sits down achingly, and both women now have their hands folded in their laps. And Connie says sadly, "We saintly types can say Og should have organized his tribe peacefully around words and civil methods. But we weren't there to see that Mog has already cut out Og's tongue and the tongues of all his people. Yes, it's a long, long story."

Kristy looks at her mother. A long anxious look. "Mom, he . . . he has the gun."

"I'm aware of that."

"He asked for it and I gave it to him."

"Mm-hmm."

"I'm sorry."

Connie snorts. "We are suckeroonies. Both of us. A suckeroonie is born every minute."

Kristy sighs.

53

H E IS INSANELY restless. Pacing the big house, a caged and teased upright beast. Little Duane trotting along behind him, sometimes ahead, sometimes circling.

Outside the FBI's cars appear and disappear and reappear like brisk generations of mushrooms, motionless, dark glassed, patient. And yesterday there was a helicopter that thwomped around in tight circles for fifteen minutes overhead, making the treetops bow and wiggle, and giving voice to the walls and to certain dishes in the cupboards.

And Robert watches himself on TV, all the fuzzy closeups of his face, always with a mustache, sometimes with the short beard, too, but never smiling. He thinks maybe if he went out there on the streets of America with a giant happy smile, nobody would recognize him.

He watches the wide-angled views of his home in Maine, the dooryard of trucks and equipment, building staging, the cattle, the pine tree, the great rise of the brown and snowy mountain behind, always blocking the setting sun.

And he sees that a camera crew has caught his older daughter, Caroline, stepping out of a friend's car, her high frothy ponytail of black hair knotted with a fake red flower. She runs for the house, hugging her head, which makes her jacket ride up. Her shape is like Kristy's. He remembered her younger. She fumbles with the doorknob. The cameras zoom in. She waves them away. They zoom in tighter on her and the door with its two-pane glass window. He has stood up. He has stepped closer to the TV. He looks around the room. His eyes rest on his new jacket, a dark wool, hanging over the back of a chair.

ROBERT AND KRISTY. In the little third-floor kitchenette. On toward midnight. The answering machine clicks as yet another message is left by yet another bewildered Pennsylvania friend. "Where are you, Kristy? Call me or Denise pronto. We are all worried."

Duane, asleep on his back on Robert's new dark wool jacket, which had fallen to the floor from the back of a chair. Duane's eyes are closed. Kristy has gotten out the canister. Big ol' canister. Pushes it across the little green table for Robert to roll one up. Robert works deftly, makes it a fat one, licks the paper, all this with one hand, his eyes on Duane. He says, "Some people know how to live."

Kristy laughs low. "The dog's life."

Robert says, "I'm goin' out. In a minute. After this. I'm goin' to hunt for somethin' real public. I want to stand there in the bright lights and let 'em see me."

Kristy drops her hands into her lap, her expression one of horror, and a little wordless squeak of protest. Then, "Please wait a little longer." She reaches and tugs on one of his fingers. "Pleeeez . . . my god, please."

"Wait for what?"

"I don't know. Just wait."

He hands her the joint, scratches a match on the book, holds the tiny faltering flame out for her. He is raised from his chair, knees bent, holding this match as she tremblingly draws the first long rich feast of smoke.

"I'll go with you," she says.

He laughs bitterly. "Afraid not, woman."

She narrows her eyes. "You can't just go out there. They're all around this block." She passes him the joint.

"I'll get through somehow. I'm good at it. I got here, didn't I? And if I don't . . . Oh well. But I'm going. I want to find a band. Dance my brains out. I wanna feel the drums inside me. Guitars 'n' stuff. Then I'll turn myself in. I'll say, 'Here's your roast, boys! Get out your spit rod.'" He draws from the dope, then holding his head way back, eyes shut, stretches out his hand with the joint for her to take it.

She stands up, ignores the joint. "I'm going. I want to be with you. I'll turn myself in, too."

He frowns, mashes the joint out in the ashtray. "Quit the shit." He steps over Duane and pulls Kristy against him. He whispers against her cheek. "Baby, baby, baby, dontcha see? There's goin' to be guns. Theirs and mine. Dontcha see? I ain't walkin' to my trial between two feds. I'm goin' to my trial in a box." He hugs her harder, laughing softly, laughing in a high, soft, unfamiliar way against her hair. She worms free.

Duane is on his feet now, yawning, looking around the room, sensing a departure, knowing the way a departure looks . . . person picking up jacket . . . person looking for his cap . . . other person running for her bag, her keys.

Robert hurries down the stairs ahead, pushing doors shut behind him. But Kristy is on his heels, doors slamming, some left ajar . . . shrieking, "God no! God no! God no! Pleeez wait . . . Robert! Pleeez, Jesus God, wait!"

In the backyard in the pink awfulness of security lights, Kristy throws herself at him, a real tackle, hard enough to make him groan. "Robert, I'll take you wherever you want to go!"

"You don't really get it, do you, baby girl?" he snarls. "You've always lived in a kinda privileged setup. Cops've been nice to you. You drive fast, they look away. You never have to worry about the thing they really hate: expired inspection stickers on an old piece a shit and havin' to be yourself a piece a shit they love to twist into a very crimpy piece a shit. You ain't never been a niggah. You don't know cops. You don't know this fuckin' socialist setup from the bottom've their boot."

"At least for god sakes stop calling it socialist, Robert. Capitalists, Robert! They are *capitalists!*"

"No difference!"

"Big difference!"

He pats her shoulder. Patronizing plus. His voice soft, sweet, but with a splintery edge. "Baby girl, you gotta figure this out. You see, you got the New World Order . . . this World Government comin' down. That's SOCIALISM. That's all there is to it."

"Socialism means government by the working people, by the proletariat! Socialism is you!"

He pats her again. Grinning weirdly.

"You stubborn redneck asshole!" she screams.

He smiles even bigger.

The pink light and the silence is so flabby—cold and thick around and between them.

A car passes on the street.

Kristy moans, "I want to die."

"Don't say that."

She is too wild and ready for fight-or-flight to have tears. She just says, "I do. And you will not get far, but I'll be right behind you because if you die I will die in my soul. I might as well be dead all over."

He almost smiles at the way she has said this. Then cocks his head and squints one eye in recollection. "You know about the MRTA militia in Peru? And the Zapatista militia in Mexico?"

"I do now."

"Those guys all work together. Not like here in this country, where everybody's got big bubblegum stuck in their ears and eyes. Militia is respected ... 'cause even sweeeeet persons got a rifle in their hand. And these guys are real slick. They take hostages and they make demands. They treat their hostages decent. I ... would like to be that way ..." He laughs. He kicks a little pebble, which rolls and wobbles several yards. "But those guys in Peru and in Mexico ... aren't like this!" He looks up at a cold, smoky mist drifting across the hellish flood of light pouring from the lamp on the Stable's gable. His voice shakes. "Not alone ... like us ... not fuckin' alone!"

55

WHEN, IN HER long bright robe, Connie finally reaches the back door to see what the commotion is, they are gone.

BACKING THE PORSCHE out onto the street, there are two government cars with tinted windows and long antennae, one car at each end of the street.

Robert just hunkers against the seat, his new knitted cap low over his eyes, his jacket collar up. Kristy takes the Porsche down a whole maze of classy side streets, and here and there other government cars are waiting for . . . for perhaps an injured man on foot. An injured man driven by a friend in a beat-up junk, a sorry truck with ratty muffler and popping manifold, old sticker, pissy luck, angry riled-up pissy luck.

"So!" says Kristy brightly. "Here we are! Out on a date! The dream date I've always dreamed of."

Robert tsks, rubs his face hard, says teasingly, "My wife always does what she's told."

Kristy cackles, "Not this one!"

He is dreadfully silent. Then, "Kristy, you are not in the real world. When your face looks like my shoulder, that is the real world."

Kristy says breathlessly, "I love to dance."

Robert says, "Fine."

Closes his eyes. Tight. For half a block. Then he looks over at Kristy's handsome profile, her small earrings, floofy short haircut, that hair almost as dark as his own. Her long pale neck. He reaches out and twists a radio knob. Gets mostly static.

"No. No."

She presses in a tape. The motion of her wrist and hand is sexy, part of her portrayal of this evening as being a date. She knows, however, that if the police grab Robert, she will jump on their backs and tear off their faces, kick them, bite them, squeeze whatever hurts most, whatever makes them let go of this pure human being, Robert Drumond. Kristy does not need a gun. Just raw woman power. Forget the prescribed features of an acceptable 1990s–Year 2000 Great Woman.

Her tape is jazz. Robert is not impressed.

She knows that under his shirt and jacket he has his Blackhawk in its holster. On the right side. The weight of it must hurt his wrecked shoulder. Even while just hanging around the house, he always has it, sometimes stuffed in his belt, but always there. During those times she has hugged him, those many many hugs, she has realized the hardness of its handle against her chest. She understands the fruitlessness of a gun to save the world, or even to save one's family, or one's self. How can it? The true enemy does not bleed! But she knows Robert, all the "whys?" of him, and there's nothing about this gun that is alien to her anymore. And in the hard unyielding ostentatiousness of that gun handle, she hears the whole story of who her father is, about Congress, which is just a tool of the corporations, which are just tools of the faceless ones. Human dignity, equality, justice, and freedom—all a lie. "Education," a farce, an enemy gun of sorts. PR of the business world. And a sea of children pressed thickly through that tiny intractable channel of academia, sports, industrial arts, and art. And herself, a human being. Not a mass-made article. Smart enough to hear it when an ordinary man's gun speaks.

When she sees the kind of place she surmises he wants, she parks the Porsche among the new pickups and shitty little cheap-made cars and locks up.

He stands by the Porsche and smokes a cigarette, intently watching cars pull in and out, people on the sidewalks, laughing and hanging in other doorways. Three times he and Kristy are held in a wash of headlights as cars enter the lot. He stares at the people getting out of their cars, moving through the grim pink Martian light of the mercury lamp by the street. Then he puts his arm around her and they walk toward the whooping, yelling, thrashing, bumpa-bumpa-bumpa barroom racket, her head on his shoulder, and once he turns her toward him with that one capable hand and kisses her hard. "I love that mouth," he growls. "It's fucking beautiful."

She sighs. "You say that word so much. Fuck. Mom and I have both noticed it."

"You and your mother talk about me a lot?"

"Oh yes." She pats his face, neatening his big mustache. And one play tap on his nose.

"What exactly do you tell each other?"

"Everything. We compare notes," she replies rather crisply.

He gets very quiet, standing there, both arms looking useless, the one that's in the sling and the other
one, too, like he has two bad arms. He says at last, "You
mad?"

She just twitches her nose.

Then they are inside. The noise of the band and the
squalling of good-timin' people is weighted, like someone
standing on your head if you were lying on the floor.
Lights flash and boil. There's one green light behind the
bar. And a supernatural-looking red light behind the band
of two electric guitars, drums, a synthesizer, a singer with
a harmonica, a singer with a tambourine, a singer gripping a mike, some women, some men, all up on a low
rough round stage, all sexy and half dressed and shaking
around, their eyes squinched shut.

The place is hot. Hotter than Kristy's attic. Hot with
dancing and clapping and howling and hopping and beer
being poured and cash being counted out into slim hands
of waitresses who wear short shorts and black stockings
and might as well be topless but for the poor little scraps
they wear on each breast, laced around the back and neck
with string as delicate as a pen line. One has glitter in her
hair. But not much is punky here. This is redneck, the
new-generation redneck, most people in their twenties
and thirties. A lot of people Kristy's age and a lot of people
turning to look at Kristy, not because they recognize her;
nobody here is part of any circle she's ever been with.
They are looking because she is as good as it gets: pale
blue eyes in dark lashes, her mouth a perfect pout, that
neck of course; with her head turning to one side, chin
high, she walks like royalty. And they check out Robert,
who still has his knitted cap low over his forehead, his

dark eyes glittering, seeing everything, like a creature that knows a trap is probably set in the tall grass.

At the table, Kristy orders a beer. Robert doesn't want anything. When the waitress is taking Robert's money, while he's paying for Kristy's beer, this waitress gives Robert the eye and he pulls the cuff of his cap up a bit, raises one eyebrow, and shouts over the racket, "Gimme one of the same!" but as the waitress walks wigglishly away in her shorts that are really short, he doesn't stare after her but looks his date in the eyes and tears off his knit cap. And he smiles for Kristy. An aren't-we-having-fun smile that shows a lot of his teeth. Nice teeth. A beautiful ordinary man.

Then he stands up and begins to work his sling off, then his jacket.

Kristy half stands, reaches across to stop his hand. He gently plucks her hand away. "Don't," she says. A word lost in the horrendous racket of the crowded club.

He grins weirdly at her as he flops the jacket over the back of his chair. And there's the shirt, yes, the camo shirt with the patch, SNOW MEN in a crescent around the abominable white hairy creature that lives in the wilderness and takes no shit. A pair of eyes at the next table fixes on Robert's rolled-up sleeve, then slides over his face, then down again to take in the way his left arm hangs, and there the tattoos, the descriptions of which rerun on every network night after night after night, day after day, like a refrain, like an ad for a product nobody needs but that you are told you must have.

Now through this dim fluttering light, another set of eyes bores right into Robert, then flicks over to Kristy, then back on Robert.

Robert's beer comes.

Kristy looks paralyzed, just staring at Robert's fingers around the tall bottle, a hand that in this dim and hellishly intermittent light, seems smaller than his actual hand. Then she looks up.

She has saved her beer for a toast. So, OK, a toast. "To the right thing!" she yells. She has tears in her eyes.

"To the left wing!" Robert yells.

"No, Robert! I said to the right THING!"

He nods.

They drink their beers up. Then order two more.

Now the waitress, reappearing in the freaky, twisted red-green light, stares at Robert as if he were much larger than he is, her eyes wide, trying to take this in, the unbelievable.

Again, when the beers arrive, they toast. Kristy hollers, "To our baby!"

Robert blinks. "What?"

"To our baby! I'm pregnant...I think. I've bought a test! A home test! Soon we'll know!"

He hangs his head. Rubs his hair.

He leans close and enunciates with lips and teeth, "So. I. Suppose. You. Are. Going. Out. And. Do. The. Mizzz thing."

She looks at him levelly. No reply.

They drink more beers. Then get up and dance. The dancing is frenetic. The music a power that makes some in this world call it the work of the devil because, you see, there are all these people losing their minds, so lacking in dignity, hopping around like fools...like witches. And sweat streams down their faces. And Robert raises his left fist and screams hoarsely, "YA-HOOOO!" and whirls around with Kristy's head held in his usual bear hug to his chest. She struggles out of this and kisses him for about two full minutes, their breathing hard through their noses as they spin around and around, attached by their mouths. This is not unusual behavior here. A lot of people act out this way one time or another. And the dim blue light swings 'round and a blinding whiteness percolates intermittently, and elbows and the fabric of a sleeve, and long hair flashing, and a locket here and there twinkles, and the glitter in the hair of a waitress passes like a small universe. These things, too, are ordinary to a good ol' bar like this. But there's something tonight that a few here know is unprecedented and far-fetched. And a certain observant few are prickly with this knowledge, bursting. Perhaps already moving toward a phone?

Between dances, as the guitarists pluck a few chords for tuning, Robert slouches in his seat, one leg raised at the knee, one leg stretched out, left hand on the table, looking around into people's faces. He smiles his nice white celebrity smile.

Robert wants *all* eyes on him; Kristy wants none. She fears his next move to get their attention. She is again paralyzed, her unspoken plea: *No, Robert, no.*

And then he and Kristy dance some more, and she is actually looking pretty damp—her hair, her big-necked stripy jersey—though her complexion is still wintry, still scared. And Robert orders two more beers, but now he looks suddenly ten years older, like a trick photo of himself, and Kristy keeps glancing at him but doesn't nag him about going. Maybe he'll just die now, of a smoker's heart switching off...a few gasps, and then die in her arms. She sees again what she saw when he was still lost in high fever, just a sprawled body, face lacking expression: that his family has a lot of Indian...maybe a grandparent...maybe his mother. She wants to ask. But he's rising from the table, with his jacket and cap and plaid sling all stuffed under his bad arm, and he shuffles over to a cigarette machine, dropping his knitted cap, which Kristy snatches up from under someone's foot. Robert punches the button for a pack of Luckies.

Kristy is so tight inside and scared. She has never been this scared in her life. And yet roused, too. Ready for the fight. When it comes.

They head for the side door, which is down a small set of stairs, and overhead the EXIT sign. Robert pushes the heavy door open and there stand five people, all seeming to be waiting for him, their eyes hard on his face. Nobody is smiling. They loosely block his way. All men. Four blacks and one waxy-looking white guy. A couple of leather jackets. One wears a weird hooded thing. Another a long black coat.

Robert's hand grabs into his shirt.

"Whoa there, Mr. Militia. We ain' pig fuzz. Mr. Famous Militia Man. We're friennn'."

This is the guy with the long coat speaking. His voice is baritone and calm, almost oozing, though he is young and not tall. His long black coat ends just above the cuffs of dark trousers and high-topped white sneakers. He has brown hair, chestnut almost. What looks like hundreds of small braids. Dark glasses. Dark brown skin. A missing front tooth. Straight backed. Very straight backed. Cat-graceful on his sneakered feet, pacing. Proud. Cocky. Points at Robert as he talks. Long fingers. No rings.

Kristy grasps the coarse camo fabric of Robert's sleeve,

hanging behind him, the great raw woman power she had hoped for now lost in a chalky dry squeak in her neck.

Not one of the stranger faces smiles. The glassy dark eyes of three of the black men look accusing. Their spokesman's dark glasses formidable. But this spokesman now touches Robert's chest lightly. Robert's eyes seem fixed on this man's essentially eyeless face, but he is soaking up the whole picture: all the faces as they stare him down, all of them with their feet apart, all of them with the confidence of armed men. The spokesman laughs, the deep, deep rich easy voice that doesn't go with his youth, his lack of height. "Gonna show them muthahs we are people, right, Mr. Militia?"

Robert barely nods.

"*We*, the people. *They*, the public servants. They get being kings and lords and muth'fuckuhs and doan 'llow us ways to get 'em out, we gotta take heads." He smiles.

Robert says, as deeply as he can, "Right."

The young guy, pivots, his long coat flaring. "You know it. I know it that we dance their dance long 'nuff. We dance an' we do. An' we hang out on the edges."

Kristy watches the waxy-looking white guy take a more restful stance, one leg bent. His hair is curly, thin on top, long. And he wears jewelry around his neck. And his leather jacket has a feather attached to a pocket zipper.

The prancing deep-voiced spokesman says, "This country's about to split wide open ... juss a mattera time, eh?" He gets quite close to Robert. In his face. He says softly, "If we're lucky."

Robert says, "You guys militia?"

The spokesman turns sharply to his left to graze his eyes over his companions. One almost smiles. A little flicker there. Spokesman turns back to Robert. "We are educators and coordinators. We gonna be sure that the next time somebody speak to one of those boys firmly, we gonna have us an army. Half a million gonna do it."

Robert blinks.

The spokesman says, "You ever hear this little talk, Mr. Militia? Find out juss what any people will quietly submit to an' you have found the exac' measure of injustice and wrong which will be impose' on them. You know the man that spoke those words?"

Robert says no.

The guy chortles. Deeply "In other words, that submittin' shit gotta go."

Robert laughs.

The guy says, "Revolution got an ugly face. But neither is life of slavery much pretty, life in the cage. A slave's life disguised as a great life suck, a slave life is a slave's life." He grips Robert's good arm. Hard. His strength, a young man's strength, just beginning. "Brother, I wish you luck in heaven."

 **57**

ND NOW THE RIDE home. Kristy watches her rearview keenly, but no one follows.

When they get back, Duane is so happy to see them both but most dutifully follows Robert upstairs, where Robert goes to his bed in the study room and lies down with his clothes on, all the windows open, and Duane curled on his chest. And Robert lies awake through the rest of the night. The whirring of his death wish subsides. No more wild rush to "surrender."

He wants to live.

58

NEXT DAY. Late afternoon. Roscoe's. A Boston nightspot. Bartender setting up, getting ready. Two guys at the bar, both older guys, both in work clothes, hearing him tell about the visitors here about an hour ago. FBI. Asking questions. Bartender, young. So blond, his blue eyes look dark. Gold earring. Black T-shirt. Wristwatch with a thick, fancy leather band. "These guys said Robert Drummond had been here last night. Had I been here last night? No, I wasn't here last night. They said, 'Aren't you Dana? We heard Dana was here last night.' I said, 'I am Dana, but I was not here last night.' They were assholes. It made me want to say, 'If I was here last night, it wouldn't do you any good because I don't talk to assholes. I got Davey and Lyle to put assholes out.' "

Both guys at the bar chuckle appreciatively. "Who *was* bartendin' here last night?" one of them asks.

"Rhonda and Ben. And these FBI goons already talked to them last night and could plainly see I was not here."

"So . . . s'pose Drummond was really here?"

Bartender leans forward on one arm, draws his free hand over his hair, and says very quietly, "He was."

"No shit."

"It was really him. He came in here with a girl. Young. Probably twenty. No trouble. They just came, did business, and went."

"Shit. So he's still around. Lotta people been thinkin' he was dead. He's worth a million if you help them catch him."

Bartender shrugs. "I don't believe that. Probably a trick."

"Yeah, probably the IRS would grab it before it reaches your hand."

"Assholes wanted me to tell them about a Porsche. Asking what I knew about a Porsche."

"A Porsche?"

"Yeah. And I said I can tell you anything you want to know about a fifteen-year-old shitbox Chevy, but you're asking the wrong person about Porsches."

"What they say?"

"They looked like I pissed them off."

"Good," one of the drinkers praises him.

"Watch out," says the other. "They'll haunt you. I don't like those turkeys. I hear too much. It's like ..." He points toward the side entrance and the cigarette machine. "Once the Russkies was their enemy. Now *we* are."

The bartender stands straight, tucking his shirt in a little neater into his belt. "The thing that really pisses me off is that those bastards probably each got a couple Porsches in their garage."

One of the drinkers narrows his eyes. "Yeah ... well ... I'm still a little confused on that Porsche business. Was they sayin' Robert Drummond was drivin' a Porsche?"

The other drinker breaks out into a high tickled hee-hee-hee. Shakes his head. "Somehow it don't fit. Militia in a Porsche." He "hee-hees" some more, sets the other two guys off laughing, too. "Like, what a world! Tomorrow ducks will be riding in Chris Crafts."

59

THE HOME PREGNANCY test comes out positive.

60

T HE CALL HAS COME. The senator, with many guards, is due for his visit to Boston night after next, in time for the dinner party. A few cars have come and gone, the cook and her staff and the housekeeper. Connie seems like a different person, worse even than schoolteacherish, her low voice efficient and machinelike as she makes the necessary calls and talks to people in the kitchen and back entrances. She has also conferred with Art about installing a lock on the door to Kristy's apartment to keep the FBI personnel from roaming when they're inside the house.

And it is understood that Robert must lie real low. And then while the senator is home, perhaps three days, Robert should "not exist" as far as anyone on the second and first floors are concerned.

But tonight, the last quiet night, Robert, in his militia shirt, sits at the head of the great long old Colonial table, a few candles lit, sweet flickering light on the antique wallpaper and on each face, and Connie is fussing over the chicken, which she has learned is Robert's favorite, and he compliments her, but still he doesn't eat much.

Grandfather clock. *Toc. Toc. Toc. Toc.*

A few clinks of a fork on china.

A passing car.

The two women, one on either side of Robert, don't even try to make nice conversation while the clock tocs and there's an impendingness of what's to come, as if what will be pushing its way in at the doors of the old brick Boston mansion will not be the senator and his caregivers but a kind of cold poisonous fog.

Robert is always a quiet eater, not slurpy or anything. But he has the unfortunate habit of picking up all his silverware—all the meticulously placed different-sized forks and spoons and knives—and tossing them into his salad dish and eating everything with one big spoon. Except chicken, which he eats with his hands. Connie watches him eat in the sweet, fluttery dark light. She can't take her eyes off his slowly rising and falling mustache, his bulging cheek. In her Russian novel, the table knows nothing but delicacy and deference to the unflexing prescriptions of social etiquette. They don't have Robert. Nor his big spoon lying across the middle of his dish. And yet his black-with-gray-bearded chin is held a little high tonight. He seems so distant and braced, all the ways those noble characters in Saint Petersburg and Moscow look by candlelight, as they prepare for war.

Robert sees her staring. His eyes change and he stops chewing.

Tonight Kristy cooked, too. A dessert. Something big and chocolate. Kristy says it is a Turkish recipe, from a friend who lived in Turkey for sixteen years. She says a few things about the lives of women in Turkey, then trails off.

Duane has chicken placed on his little dish, but like always, it's gone so fast, he just stares at everyone from his chair, hopping from foot to foot, coaxing.

Robert reaches over to pat Duane, who ducks his head, trying to lick the chicken grease off Robert's fingers.

The grandfather clock makes a sound, a soft enk sound, readying itself to chime.

Robert squares his shoulders, moving his eyes over Kristy's face, then her dark sweater top, then her hands. Then down to his own hands, one to each side of his plate. Spoon in the plate.

Phone pulses its cheap new-age pulse-pulse pulse-pulse. Clock chimes eight times while Connie pushes her chair back and bustles to the kitchen.

Robert keeps his eyes on his hands and plate.

Kristy asks Robert to pass the salad.

He does.

On the phone a voice explains rather dully to Connie that this is the Federal Bureau of Investigation calling from a car phone out on the street, hates to interrupt her evening, needs to talk with her and her daughter . . . has already spoken with some of her household staff—he doesn't say which ones; she doesn't ask. He needs to talk now. Right now. "Can you open your gates." Grammatically this is a question, but not in tone.

Connie hangs up on him. The wrong thing. You do not hang up on the FBI. What is the right thing to say to them to make them go away?

She reappears at the dining-room door from the back hall, looking across the full length of the room at Robert, who has pushed his plate ahead and now grips his face with his hands. His hair, thinning at the temples, notice-able when he covers his face.

Kristy is dabbing at something she has spilled on her sleeve.

Toc toc toc toc.

Connie goes over to the back of Kristy's chair. "Do you want to serve your dessert now, Kristina?"

Kristy pushes her chair back, carries away a few dishes.

Connie covers the chicken platter and rounds up salad bowls, china that is older than anyone in this room. China that has worn well. Not at all weary. Not at all sick of the farce. And Connie says to Robert, "That was the FBI. They are out front of the house right now, at the gates. They want to come in and talk."

61

RT'S WIFE IS NOT HOME from work yet. Art watches the news, gripping the channel flicker for dear life, like he may need very badly to stop the man from talking, the man being briefly interviewed, Senator Phil Balonsky. The senator has been asked to comment on the fact that hundreds of Militia Movement people are demanding that Robert Drummond be publicly flogged before he is put to death.

Before the array of mikes, Senator Balonsky's hand flutters dismissively. "Can we presume we live in a civilized nation?"

He turns to his far left and a correspondent calls out, "So you are saying, Senator, that being flogged is . . . torture?"

Senator Balonsky's eyes twinkle. And then he laughs. "Can we all agree on that?"

The same correspondent calls out, "Senator, if flogging is torture, then what is death by hanging?"

Without missing a beat, the senator leans into the mikes. "A deterrent."

Art lays the channel flicker down very slowly on the coffee table, and he stands up, his face expressionless, and walks out to the kitchen and picks a plastic bottle out of a pretty little square basket of plastic bottles and pens and Scotch tape, and he shakes into his hand six Tums.

62

NEXT EVENING. Two agents briskly cross the street to the front door of an apartment building. They scan the names printed beside the door-buzzer buttons.

ARTHUR BERRY

For two hours they will question, nag, and insinuate threat. Insinuate reward. Then back to threat.

Both Arthur and Mary Berry will seem "kinda dense."

OK, a polygraph. Some hypnosis. And lots more "chat." Appointments will be made for first thing tomorrow morning. A few more insinuations of threat.

Before the agents reach the street, Art will chomp down a lotta Tums. Which do nothing for his stomach fire and shortness of breath. He goes to bed early.

He wakes up within an hour. Scared. He whispers, "Heavenly Father, whatever they do to me, give me even just a little portion of Your strength. Amen."

EVENING DARKNESS. Attractive old-fashioned yellowish gaslight-looking lamps light all the brick walks outside. Cars cover every inch of bricked driveway around the Stable, and then more cars pull up through the open gates and stop at pathways, and people step out, car doors closing softly, the way all doors open and close for the elite. Hard heels clopping along. Bitter laughter. Small talk. Breezy talk. Optimism light and bright as helium. Someone whose job it is just to answer the door and to take coats is doing that job two floors down, almost directly below Robert Drummond, who lies alone in the near dark, on his back on his narrow bed, shirtless, one knee up, spinning the cylinder of his Blackhawk with soft, sensuous clicks, hammer back, half cocked. He hears Duane downstairs yapping. He hears another carload show up. He hears music. A piano. The one in the big room off the dining room. It plays a concerto. Although Robert wouldn't be able to tell you it was a concerto. Nor does he give a shit what it's called.

He is thinking only of the *thing* that has entered this

sturdy home, the thing that has destroyed his people, has destroyed the lives of billions, smashed all hope of democracy, of the very sovereignty "the fathers" died for, and now this thing walks with arrogance through the halls of every capitol and now has entered this sweet, sweet intimate space. What finally does Robert Drummond intend? Has he had another change of heart?

THE SENATOR SITS in his armed chair at the head of the long table, which he loves to do. Connie has always called it his "Dad thing." And he is being served a choice of breads by one of the cook's staff—or "maid," as others less liberal would call her. And, always gracious with household personnel, he nods to her before she steps back. He is smiling and laughing with the guest at his right but he is worried. He is, in fact, disoriented by what the FBI has come to suspect about his daughter and Robert Drummond.

His daughter, Kristina, sits near him, two seats away, next to the wife of federal judge Frederick Ramsey. Kristina is wearing a long, low-necked, long-sleeved, very becoming emerald dress. Her lovely neck! Her perfect hair. Her eyes bright with the candles, her teeth creamy with the glow of the Colonial-era candelabra. There is a red mark on her neck. Looks like a hickey. Could it be a hickey? She'd wear a high collar if it was. She is socially exquisite. She has been a regular princess since she was only four. Things will work out for Kristina. The senator is sure of this. He is not worried. He never dwells on her little spells, her revolts, her obsessions, and now her little confusion about her career. And now this crazy possibility of the Drummond thing . . . like Patty Hearst or something.

Both the Bureau and the Boston police have advised him not to be here tonight. Not in Boston. And especially not in this house. And he watches how impatient his wife is with the layers of FBI here since this afternoon. FBI in every nook, cranny, and shrubbery. She used to be so good-natured about security men. Now . . . what's up, Connie?

She is seated down at the far end of the table, with some of the people he knows she always gets a kick out of, and her deep, throaty, but publicly restrained laughter rises from the interstices of bright conversation that this room is charged with tonight. The senator is actually glad to be here. He loves the smell of this home, a little damp, a little musty. Quite Boston. And he loves Connie. He loves everything about Connie, even though she frustrates him. He especially loves her secret self, her funny, smart, nonpublic self, and everything they have lived. Everything.

The senator is a tall man, with a long clean-shaven face and long lower jaw. A ready smile. One front tooth has an odd discoloration, but this has been a kind of trademark for him. In the world of plastic people, in the halls of $3,000 suits, $30,000 hair transplants, $2,000 gym-membership-trim waists, Jerry Creighton's tooth makes him seem like a kind of charming pirate.

He has blue, interesting eyes and bushy brows and hair that was dark once. He is known as, yes, "the Liberal," which means he works hard for the rights of blacks and gays and women and foreigners who have graduated from Harvard . . . or Yale . . . or the like . . . and he works hard for the rights of Big Business, as does the rest of Congress. Even if Big Biz doesn't own you, you would identify. Right? Does a bear shit in the woods? Does Congress groan and sweat in a one-piece, muscular, very oily choreography to give the corporations what they so desire? Aren't inalienable rights a commodity like ice cream? Like justice? Like time? Like health? Like shelter? Like freedom? Like dignity? A sad, sad fact of life. He would not say it was good. Just unstoppable. Even the great Heavenly Powers of Good can never change the facts of life, can they?

Meanwhile, upstairs on the third floor, Robert Drummond sits on the edge of the bed, revolver in his good hand, staring at his camo shirt tossed over a wicker chair next to a four-foot glossy red Buddha. He stares at the patch of his militia. The white creature, grinning. Robert stands up. Walks to the wicker chair.

The senator is thinking that having Phillip Loring here, the lobbyist from the Parks Group, is critical to his upcoming campaign, and Connie knows this and he knows she has tried to make everything perfect tonight. Loring's cohorts and too many other big men will be hearing about certain things that might be agreed to tonight after this dinner.

The senator again glances over at the small scarlet mark on his daughter's neck. He feels for his fork. But the meal is fried chicken. He stares at the chicken. Everybody seems to love the chicken, dabbing their mouths with their dinner napkins drawn up from their laps and pushing their fingers through their napkins roughly like garage mechanics cleaning up after a job.

He hates chicken. She knows he hates chicken and never lets any of the cooks bother him with it.

Huge bunches of chrysanthemums are everywhere. Too huge. White. Like a funeral home. Alternated with giant buckets of poinsettias that are real but always seem to Jerry to be artificial. And what's this with the papier-mâché reindeer and turkeys in the front entry hall? Kinda hokey. A lot of things about this evening could make him feel edgy if he weren't already edgy.

Robert Drummond buttons up the shirt, tucks it into his pants, meticulously, redoing his belt. The piano playing has stopped. For some reason. Whatever these people have for reasons.

The senator tries a roll. Chews. He sees that his guests all seem to be unaware of any oddness here. And maybe they are all a bit titillated over the danger factor, the making-history factor, of being here in Boston with Robert Drummond still at large. Judge Ramsey is bragging that he could beat Bob Kane's wife arm wrestling—a joke— but he actually slams his elbow up on the table and wiggles his brows at her as if to dare her.

The senator looks again at Kristina, just as Phil Loring is beginning a quietly eager chat with him about MAI, the slick media-silent Multilateral Agreement on Investment, which will give humongous business interests vast unchallengable powers over countries, states, communities, and all forms of life. The senator sees his daughter's blue eyes are more bright, even more blue than he's ever seen them.

And now as his beloved, sandy-haired Constance comes over to Mrs. Ramsey and leans to ask something that will make Mrs. Ramsey feel special and grand, the senator notices Connie's tasteful gray dress has a conservatively high neck on it.

Now as Connie stands straight, squaring her shoulders so that her great bustline perks up, he sees in her green eyes a happiness . . . no, not happiness exactly, but a proud savagery—lioness, she-wolf, or maybe a wild mare.

And when she comes around to the very end of the table, he wags a finger for her to bend down to him with her ear, and she leans down and places her hand on his hand and he whispers, "You are ravishing tonight."

And she thanks him in an oddly pale voice, and he feels a stab of fear, fear of loss, years gone, many things. Gone.

She straightens up, throws out her chest again, and her eyes scan the room. She is putting off a wonderful womanly, warm powdery smell, something from the past, something probably no longer on the market but that she may have kept from girlhood. Maybe it was her aunt's.

Connie prowls along back to her seat, after having a few words with the Davidsons and Myra Jackson, and she looks back across the crystalline clutter of the long table into the wide eyes of her daughter, who stares back a moment, then looks away, back to the chat she's having with Mrs. Ramsey.

Robert Drummond flicks the new lock open, steps into the hall at the top of the attic landing, revolver in his hand, arm straight down, the muscles of that arm simmering under the effulgence of his tattoos, his face muscles locked and wooden.

Warm breads are brought to the table, yeast and corn. And beer bread. Very nice.

Connie hears Duane digging at something splinterishly, and so she pushes her chair back again and goes into the back hall and finds that he is intent on getting upstairs. He now flings himself at this door with all four feet. Two young FBI men smile from where they stand by the entryway bench. Connie scolds Duane, then shoves him into the farthest parlor, closes the door. She returns to the dining room as another bottle of show-off Château Latour is brought to the table by the cook's youngest staff member, Heidi, buoyant and bouncy in a thin sort of way, who hurries back to the kitchen.

Robert Drummond reaches the next-to-last step at the bottom. All around him the figures of 1770s people and animals and trees in a custard-colored wallpaper universe. He knows if this door was open, he would see the senator's face at the end of the table in the dining room across the hall. He knows he has six cartridges in the cylinder, no safety. The idea is to disengage the latch of this door easy careful, then kick it wide, Blackhawk raised. He knows there may be people in the way. People he cares about. And if this happens, he will shove past and with everyone off guard and openmouthed, they will not understand what's happening. He has "the Liberal" fucker one way or the other.

Connie turns smiling at this scintillating warm scene of breads and messy napkins and drunken eyes and funny faces. People here are good people. Some she has known for years. Earnest people. Tender, funny people. But... there is so much that she hears them say that makes her know they have never seen "it," the truth. Forgive them, for they know not what they do.

A motion catches her eye, back at the door in the rear hallway, the shadow of someone moving in a skulking way. She blinks. She sees the shadow move again. Now an arm. A young man in a three-piece suit hovering out there. Another FBI fellow. And she sees that Jerry keeps looking over at her with a kind of shrewd, sad squint.

This morning it was announced on every network that Robert Drummond was seen by multiple witnesses in a nightclub on Friday with a dark-haired young woman. The young woman drove a Porsche. Nothing about a license plate number.

Connie returns to the table, where her old friend Myra Jackson offers to pour her a glass of the Château Latour, which is so red it is almost black. Connie says, "Thank you, sweetie! Yessssss, indeedy. I would like a glass. Fillll it." But she keeps her eye on the young man in the hall.

Beyond the closed door, Robert Drummond still stands on the next-to-bottom step, Blackhawk raised, hammer raised full cock over the loaded chamber, his eyes no longer eyes Connie or Kristy would recognize, no longer soft, no longer playful, not even angry, just cold.

He remembers in a subliminal way the hard squeeze of the young black outside the bar, the man's extraordinary voice saying, "That submittin' shit gotta go."

Now he hears, not subliminally, but actually and vividly, Kristy's laugh. It is not a thing you hear often. Her laugh is a low, lovely bray. . . .

His eyes fill with tears that make the closed door look wiggly. His throat clenches. His arms prickle, the blood of life returning, that suffusion of empathy which some call God, some call weakness. He lowers the gun.

65

THAT NIGHT in their big bed in the near darkness, Jerry urges his wife to come back to Washington and bring Kristy there for their mother-daughter time together.

She says, "Oh, Jerry. I'm tired. Let's hash it out tomorrow."

He takes her hand. As if to propose. He gently rubs her fingers. "Connie, between you and me, I know how...how sympathetic you can be to the underdog. And how...how deeply moved Kristina is by this world."

She says nothing, and he continues to caress her fingers, this the hand that wears the rings that he had bought for her, thirty-three years ago almost in a frenzy, charged with love—one of the few times in his life that he was reckless...effusive...fire-eater...hippity-hop. Now in another voice, "Drummond is a screwball...a psychopathic crazed ultra-extremist Nazi nutcase. He is dangerous. This is different, Connie. This isn't indigent artists, welfare mothers, or homeless bag ladies. This is something very bad...for all of us."

She says nothing. He takes a *very* deep breath. "Tell me, Connie. You can tell *me*. Did you see an injured man around here the evening after Kip Davies was killed? What do you know? And is the Porsche girl Kristy?"

She says nothing.

He says, "I've been meeting with John Talma, the FBI guy in charge of all this. I have a lot of respect for Talma. He says you do know something. You act suspicious. Do you realize you are giving this impression?"

She says nothing. She just closes her fingers around his hand.

He says, "It's delicate for him. Because of who you are. But he has...his instincts. He's one of the best, Connie. He's been with the Bureau for years. He's seen a lot. And the fact remains, all signs of Drummond ended at our gates. And now maybe *inside* our gates. The Bureau wants to know why the floor was recently painted in the Stable. Can you tell me that? If you won't, they'll be talking with Art again tomorrow."

She says nothing.

He puts his arms around her. She breathes against his neck. He says, "If you and Kristy don't come back with me, I think I am going to have a heart attack."

She just breathes.

He holds her tighter. A small cautious kiss on her forehead. "Think about it, Connie. Tomorrow is a new day."

66

Two days after the senator is gone, a UPS driver carries a nice, good-feelin' box to the workbench in the Stable. Art signs for it. The UPS truck leaves in a brisk, tumbling, hollow-sounding roar.

The box is for Kristy. It is a guitar. A worn, old acoustic with an intricately embroidered strap. And a book of songs. And a note on pretty stationery.

> Dear Professor Creighton,
> I hope you remember me. I was in Professor Garrett's seminar during the conference and I will never forget your lecture. It has changed my life. You mentioned playing guitar and I want you to have this one that was my dad's. But I can't play worth peanuts. I wanted to give you something that would show you how much you gave me with your words.
> Love,
> Shelly Sykes

No return address.

Kristy will open this package. She will not remember

Shelly Sykes. She will not remember mentioning playing the guitar at any recent seminars. She is a fairly good pianist. But guitar? She has played guitar. When she was a teenager. But she never thinks of it now. Never. This is quite odd. Probably the student got her mixed up with Nancy Pfeiffer. Kristy will strum the guitar a moment, find it is nicely tuned, she'll halfheartedly pick a half-remembered melody. Then she will stand the instrument against the love seat with its fretted neck showing beyond the chair's arm like a fist, or like the head of a mythic creature, raising from liquid mists, alert. Alert and listening.

67

ROBERT IS BACK in the big bed eating salty gourmet crackers from a box while Connie reads to him. It is now decided and, perhaps a little too carelessly planned, that tomorrow she will warm up the Mercedes, her Mercedes, pack two nice sandwiches, which will most likely not be eaten, put Duane into his purple harness— and Duane does surely love to ride—and then she will drive Robert Drummond up the Mass Turnpike, on up and up and up, up to Maine, to his home. She knows though he doesn't say it that this is what he wants.

And so now, what she does is read to him some scenes from the Russian novel.

And then she plops the big book onto the floor and she leans over toward Robert and she puts one hand on each of his shoulders, including the one that is scarred badly and almost solidly colored in tattoo ink, and he sets the cracker box aside thinking she wants to play bear or caveman or bull or chicken or one of those things, but then sees her eyes have tears and yet she's laughing a little, and she recites in her deepest, grandest voice, " 'Oftentimes, to win us to our harm, The instruments of darkness tell us truths; Win us with honest trifles, to betray's In deepest consequence.' " She sighs sadly. "That one was for me."

He looks uncomfortable. And something sets off his smoker's cough, which makes his face red and his eyes water. And he laughs apologetically.

And she laughs. She now folds her hands on the blanket over her lap. "Here's one for you, my love. 'To thine own self be true, And it must follow, as the night the day, Thou canst not then be false to any man.' "

He says, "Thanks." Then snorts, again flushing. This stuff embarrasses him.

She puts up a hand. "Wait! One more. 'This goodly frame, the earth, seems to me a sterile promontory; this most excellent canopy, the air, look you, this brave o'erhanging firmament, this majestical roof fretted with golden fire, why, it appears no other thing to me than a foul and pestilent congregation of vapours!' "

He has stared the whole time at her hand, seeing more of the universe in her hand than in the genius of Shakespeare, but then says with a little pleasant hop of his shoulders, "That's neat," and looks cautiously at her face.

And she says, " 'Most friendship is feigning, most loving mere folly.' "

He looks over at Duane, who has gone mercifully to sleep on Connie's pillow against the headboard. Then he looks back at Connie and he has hard worry around his eyes seeing that her eyes are welling up, and he pushes the blankets around a bit and makes her a nice nest and reaches to one-handedly fuss some of her sandy, squiggly hair behind both ears, then fusses around some more with the nest of blankets and sheets and tells her to curl into them with her thick legs and soft hips, but instead of kissing her throat as he surely loves to do or climbing onto her, he just hides his face against her throat, saying, "I'm sorry. I'm really sorry."

68

THE PHONE. Three twenty-two by the bedside clock, the smell of Robert Drummond all over her, Connie reaches for the receiver, places it too slowly to her ear. "Yes?"

It is Jerry. But it doesn't sound like Jerry. His voice is oddly high and tight. "Constance. Tell me. Is he in the house? Is Robert Drummond in our house?"

She laughs. Not a very good laugh. There are times she can be quite a good actress. But not this laugh. This laugh is all wrong.

Robert moves beside her. His foot. An unintended hurting scratch against her ankle from his toenails.

Jerry says, "It would be in all of our interests if you let the FBI inside now. There is a deal. You let them in now and they'll report that you and Kristina were hostages."

Again Connie laughs. Almost a hoot.

Jerry says, "A few more hours. Then they are coming in. They have all the necessary warrants. They have had warrants since Tuesday but have been generous ... have been...friendly to us. Use your brain not your heart, Connie. I trust you to do this...the right thing. Quietly. No need for bull horns and tear gas...or...me coming back and giving the media a show. Everything is at stake, Connie. Everything. For once. This isn't the stage."

69

OUTSIDE, JOHN TALMA and the others, all ears, all eyes. Ready to make a move. Giving it a few more hours. A really bad situation. A few more hours. Maybe the world will end and everything will take care of itself. A few more hours. Hear that rustle and wait. Hear that guitar that whispers to them with its crackling voice the coveted truth. Some people are crazy. Creighton's women, crazy crazy crazy. What a high-hoopin' media circus this one will be when it finally gets out.

70

THE DAY IS GRAY and the Mercedes's windshield is deeply tinted, but Robert Drummond wears dark glasses. Metal frames. The cop kind. Also, see there, pulled down to his eyebrows his knitted black watch cap and dark jacket so nondescript as he slouches way down in the velvety seat, Duane on his lap.

Art stands directly in front of the glinting Mercedes grille staring into that shadowed spot of Robert's face as Connie backs the car out. Art keeps both hands in the pockets of his jeans. No wave.

Connie is straining her head, neck, and shoulders to see anything coming up the street. Robert does not look for her, just keeps looking down across his chest at nothing. There are no cars on this street. None.

Connie wears a pair of ivory-colored leather-palmed knit gloves and Jackie Kennedy–style dark-frame sunglasses and a camel hair coat, and dressed so conservatively, half believes, in some skewed way, that if need be, she can protect Robert with influence. Which is, at this moment, luminously true.

UPSTAIRS, KRISTY does not look out the window. She lies on Robert's narrow bed, her face a mess, a swollen horrid mess, and now more shoulder-racking sobs as she hears the iron gates clang shut.

OH, JESUS GOD, what is this on the next street?

On both sides of the street, a sprawl of government cars, vans, and cop cars, and in between them clusters of men in bullet-proof black. And helmeted. Guns ready. Riot guns, handguns, and rifles. All standing there. No one doing anything. Just standing there, watching hard, watching the Mercedes pass . . . having just received the order, hearing only ten minutes ago via the bugged guitar, Kristy and Robert hugging good-bye, Kristy weeping, Kristy shrieking, Kristy whispering his name over and over and over. Only ten minutes ago, orders changed in the blink of an eye. *On the other end. In Maine. Without the senator's heated-up women. Without the senator's CON-CERNS. We simplify.*

They just stand there like a kind of awed audience of adoring fans on both sides of the street and the sidewalks for two blocks as the Mercedes slides sweetly between them.

One agent shakes his head.

And then the Mercedes comes to the blocked-off area, but these gentlemen, lowering their walkie-talkies, seeing the Mercedes coming slowly toward them, stand aside, what seems like a whole platoon of roadblock cops standing aside with the light of day reflected off the Mercedes grille rippling across their faces, helmets, padded chests, shotguns, and gloved hands.

And now through a narrow tunnel between media vans, and cameras, cameras rolling, media people not as spellbound as the cops. Media humming.

And now the Mercedes turns onto another side street, then another. And then normalcy.

Connie keeps her stately senator's wife posture and expression, tipping the wheel with her gloved hands, eyes ahead.

After they ride awhile—through the rest of the city that bangs and shimmers and screeches like a beast with no head, no body, just jaws, then out of the city, which is still really city, still gritty, still rusty, but more parking lots, less upper stories—Connie takes off her gloves.

She adjusts the heater a bit. Duane looks around happily at other cars, yards passing by. Though he had especially enjoyed all the cops. Now no cops. But he loves these tollbooth people. Robert grips Duane's harness to keep him in line at tollbooths. The tollbooth people don't look in at Robert and Duane. Sometimes they don't even look at Connie. They just stick out a hand with a ticket in it.

Now and then cops. A lotta cops. They drive fast on the highway. Speed limits aren't for cops. Even when they're just considering the next exit to find a donut shop. Robert doesn't seem to be looking out the window enough to see cops, but Connie thinks maybe Robert can feel them, like an old man feels rain in his bones.

Now they ride and ride. And there's no music played. No radio. No tapes. No Shakespeare. No questions. Connie's questions all answered. Her head, heart, and guts cold and shaky with new knowledge.

Robert starts looking out his window a little bit. Yeah,

he is homesick. But now behind him he has spread himself around some. And now backward he will yearn as well. He will never see the face of the child, though Kristy tells him she has no intention of aborting it. She is already getting little clothes for it. Toys. Plans. And beautiful highfalutin' names.

On into New Hampshire, there are snowbanks of respectable size.

Connie suggests Robert eat a sandwich.

"No thanks, dear. I'm kinda . . . not hungry yet."

"Me, neither."

He looks at her.

A cop cruiser whisks past, antennae wagging, tires throwing up a little road slush.

She looks over at Robert, who is pressed as deeply into the seat back as he can get. This man who was husband, who was father, who was provider, who was neighbor, until "they" broke him. Yes, "they" pulled the strings. He pulled the trigger. It is done. The order can no longer be reversed. His home is of course being watched by "them." "They" are waiting. Will he manage to have a word with his teenaged son? Hold his wife and daughters? Call up his brothers and sisters for a quick visit? Will he stand with bowed head as they cuff him, hands jerked behind his back, his damaged shoulder white-hot with pain? Or will he have a shoot-out with them and die there in his home with the anxious cattle and the pine tree? Will some of his family die, too? Faithful to the end? The evidence of their love folded up and vanished into the steaming CS gas and inevitable, in fact, well-calculated FBI-induced flames. By tonight the networks will be blazing with footage of these last images, images that Connie does not ever want to see.

And the teachers had ordered him to stand and he stood, with all eyes on him, the eyes of his peers.

Had he really tried to please the teachers?

Should he have?

To thine own self be true, And it must follow, as the night the day, Thou canst not then be false to any man.

The Mercedes enters Maine. Duane licks Robert's face.

Connie is now thinking about birds.

The Mercedes eventually takes roads that bear northwest, two-lane tar roads, passing little stores with gas pumps at junctions, strip developments of homes decked out for Christmas, snowmobile dealers, car dealers, then trafficky towns with IGAs. And then between towns again. Great stretches. A lot of pine trees.

Connie is still thinking about birds. How when you find one with a broken wing, you keep it a while. Or a raccoon that was hit by a car. How you keep it a while and get attached. You give it a name. Rocky, if it's a raccoon.

The hills of Robert's home have high, chunky banks of snow and power lines that zigzag across the narrow roads.

He tells her she can let him off at "the foot" of his road when they get there.

She says fine.

Duane hops up, front paws on the dash, his eyes lightning quick, taking in the otherworldliness of what he sees.

And so now they have arrived in Robert's town, which is actually a lot of paper company land and investment corporation land, miles of stone walls, trees, occasional groupings of new homes, new and old trailers, old farmhouses and barns and farmland no longer farmed. And there a working sandpit. And there an abandoned sandpit, grown along the fringes in saplings. All snow.

And now an intersection of two narrow roads, four equal parts of hilly rocky woods and field. This is "the foot" of Robert's road. No road signs. Not even stop signs. No yield. No merge.

There is a fogginess over a pond in one of the snowy fields, the pond not yet frozen on one end. Perhaps a swirling spring. The mountains are close, prickly looking with gray purplish hardwoods and the dark green of pines and fir and spruce and hemlock. And birch. Resplendent. White and silver. And so much snow. So much.

She thinks, as he opens the door and stands outside there a minute with the door hanging open, lighting a cigarette, that this is what you must do when the wild creature is ready. You return it to the woods. It will probably die soon, in some ugly way, but that is not your business.

Duane wants to get out with Robert so Robert lets him get out, and waits while Duane pees on things and sniffs around, and then Robert shoves the little dog back inside, presses the door shut.

And Robert starts walking fast.

And Connie is thinking that nature sucks, it really does, but you have to trust Mother Nature, that in the long run, she knows what she's doing.

And just like you'd expect, Robert turns once and looks back, then turns away again and starts running for home.

I think I am a good man,
but . . . all over the world
they say I am a bad man.

—Geronimo